Order of The White Rock

Book Two of The Unity Chronicles

GRAHAM MANN

Chapter 1 - Injis

Wild Space: Five years before the activation of The Unity Spire.

"Unleash The Hunger," barked Injis. A single missile screamed from the weapons array and ripped through the nebulous gases of Wild Space. The weapon's payload grew impatient, eager to be released as it drew ever closer to its stricken target. The missile detonated in a violent burst of light and shrapnel, just metres from the hull of the Scavenger ship. The magnetised liquid contents were unremarkable and benign in appearance, but once set free, the liquid stuck fast to the vessel's dense, metallic, surface and immediately went to work. The Hunger ate through the ship's hull with a ravenous intensity. The defenceless Scavenger ship was being devoured before the wide, terrified eyes of the Scavengers who had once called it their home and prison. The few that had refused to join Injis's army were left onboard the ship to experience the wrath of her savage new weapon first hand. Injis had freed the Scavengers from their icy cell in the Zeta

Belt and towed them beyond the edge of the known galaxy, deep into Wild Space. She had used their fear and disorientation cruelly against them. Injis offered them a choice. Join her to conquer the galaxy and end the Protector Droids, or to take their chances marooned in their wreck of a ship. A number of the Scavengers believed that the Protector Droids, (the beings who had facilitated their incarceration), were indestructible, and that Injis was a fool to even plan to contemplate in attacking them. These doomed souls had stayed onboard the ship to unwittingly become victims of The Hunger's boundless appetite.

The merciless display of destruction was intended to be a demonstration of Injis' power, and it served its purpose perfectly. Soon enough, the bodies of those who had remained aboard drifted out of the breached hull... their frozen corpses floated in the vacuum of space, faces locked in agonising screams of panic and terror. Within an hour the bodies were all that remained. All traces of the Scavenger ship were gone, consumed by Injis's merciless weapon. She hadn't needed to utter a single word. The surviving Scavengers whom she had forced to witness the vulgar display of power, were already on their knees. They pledged their allegiance to her, heads bowed, ready to receive the Mark of the Flame. The mark was a brand of sorts - which was burned almost painlessly into the skin of the nape. Those who wore the Mark of the Flame willingly had sworn undying loyalty to Injis. Phase one was complete. The Scavengers were under her control, but they were an imperfect tool. Vicious and callous enough, but they needed to be shaped into warriors. Time however was on Injis' side. Even she wasn't foolish enough to take on The Hushed. She would play the long game, and when the time was right, she would take back what was rightfully hers.

Chapter 2 - Sin

Decommissioned Industrial Asteroid Sin: Eight days before Activation of The Unity Spire.

Tam sat inside the crude lean-to he'd fashioned from rusted sheet metal and scraps of wire when he'd first discovered this relative haven. He had constructed the shelter inside an abandoned warehouse which provided him with breathable air, clean water and a plentiful, (if not particularly varied), supply of canned and vacuum-packed food. There was also an abundance of thick cloth sacking, which although coarse and itchy, afforded a much better level of comfort and warmth than the bare concrete floor. The warehouse was far enough away from the bustle and sleaze of the main stretch that it was quiet, secure and inconspicuous. No one ventured this far out, even though it was barely beyond the boundary of the Biodome.

Tam had been sent to Sin against his will and had been left no choice but to call this hell hole his home. He had been displaced from everything he knew and had ever loved. Like it or not, the fact remained that this was Tam's home now, and an ex industrial asteroid in the Yetu regions was a difficult place to exist. The Yetu region crawled with a colourful array of vicious and deadly low lives, insidious gangsters, scavengers, pirates, dealers, slavers and thieves. All manner of deviance and scum frequented this remote corner of space. At times, Tam believed it would've been better to have perished on Veela VI at the hands of the Feruccian filth, than to live through this waking nightmare. Yet his parents had felt this to be the best course of action. They had told Tam that if he managed to escape Veela VI and survived, the legacy of his race would live on. *Selfish bastards*, were the words that echoed inside his brain. Better he had died with them -- none the wiser to the bigger picture, which had unfolded to become even more grim than anyone could ever have imagined. However, his people had decided that they must live on, and they had embedded in him the means to do so. It was allegedly *'The greatest honour ever bestowed upon any Veel'aan. You should feel as proud as we do'*. These were the parting words of his parents. There wasn't an ounce of consideration for him in that decision, and now he hated them for what they had done. He had been condemned to a life where he, as the last of his people, had been tasked with the preservation of his race. How was he supposed to preserve and rebuild his species on his own? It had been difficult enough just to survive here. *If this was their grand plan, then maybe they deserved to die, the idiots.* His thoughts were clouded by seething anger.

There was only one thing that eclipsed Tam's anger at his parents; the unbridled rage he felt for the House of Royals. For generations, his people had selflessly and lovingly served them. They had bestowed gifts of jewellery and precious handcrafted trinkets upon them, dressed them in finery and hosted great banquets in their honour. The Royals had gorged themselves on the fine food and wine that had been prepared in their honour. The Veel'aans danced, performed and turned tricks for the Royal's amusement. Despite all that the Veel'aans had given in their service, had the Royals come to his people's aid in their hour of need? No. Did they strike down, in the name of rage and vengeance, those who had slaughtered their most loyal friends and allies? Again, a resounding NO! These thoughts consumed him. He pictured the Royals, sat smugly in the finery they had been gifted, surrounded by the luxurious decor that had also been bestowed upon them, safe in the knowledge that they were protected by their army of Protector Droids. As far as Tam was concerned, the Royals were as much to blame as the Ferrucians. They might as well have killed his people themselves. His thoughts switched back to his parents. He was bewildered by their thought processes. What had they expected him to do? Tam was certainly not a one-man army, about to take on the whole galaxy in the name of his people. He was a scrawny twenty-two-year-old with an antiquated blaster and a homemade knife. Even the blaster was scavenged from the Junker's yard, and its reliability was questionable at best. In this moment, his only concern was to simply stay alive and find a way to get off this forsaken rock.

Tam had spent hours monitoring the comings and goings of numerous species and ships. He scratched notes onto scraps of paper to keep an accurate record. The activity of the ships had, (up until recently), been sporadic and unpredictable at best. Over the last few weeks however, a vessel named the Gift Horse had developed a pattern to its visits. The ship was eerie looking and antiquated, an ancient battle-scarred wooden galleon, held together with metal bolsters and plating. She had been space-proofed with robust shielding. In stark comparison to her appearance, the bizarre vessel was powered by state-of-the-art quad ion engines. The captain of this oddment was Kraddich, a salty old relic from a forgotten era. His crew of pirates and smugglers operated mainly in the outer regions. They had taken to visiting here every second week, drinking, gambling and telling tales of their latest plunders. The captain and his crew were frequent visitors to the bars and pleasure suites of the asteroid, which apart from the vast array of narcotics, were the only real reason to visit this hapless rock. If these questionable establishments had offered a loyalty scheme, then the pirates would be living off freebies for eternity. Their visits had become like clockwork, totally uncharacteristic for a ramshackle rabble such as pirates. Tam had seen a chance. If he could stow away on that ship, he could be free of this place, and find somewhere to start anew in more civilised surroundings... if he didn't get discovered and sold into slavery.

But what did he have to lose? Nothing, was the correct answer to that question. His existence couldn't possibly get any worse than it was right now. *At least slaves got fed and sheltered by their masters.* Tam really had hit an all-time low, debating slavery versus his current existence. He had taken to talking to himself over the years, which was understandable, considering there was only one person he'd encountered in his timeline here who he deemed worthy of his attention. That person was Neela; she had been his beacon of hope in the dark times he had endured. Neela worked a pleasure suite named Lust, not by choice, but rather as a necessity. She had told Tam many times.

"My body is my own to do with as I must. Though never forget my heart and mind are yours alone that I choose to give." He couldn't bear the thought of Neela being mauled, kneaded and used by the scum that visited the asteroid, for their self-gratification. Yet he knew she had no choice, it was her only means of survival. His heart broke every time she left, only to return to him a physically broken version of herself, shattered, bruised, but never devoid of spirit and optimism. When he found a way to get aboard the Gift Horse and get out of here, taking Neela with him was an essential part to any future plan.

Tam had been caught up in his thoughts for far too long. The planet Tah and its moons shone in piercing blue-green hues through the jagged opening of the warehouse's wrecked outer roof. This told him that it was the small hours of the morning and Neela really should've been back by now. His worry got the better of him. In a fit of panic, he pulled the thick cloth hood of his robe over his head, and left the comparative comfort and safety of his lean-to and headed for the unpredictable streets, bars and pleasure suites that he so despised.

Chapter 3 - The Player

Treelo sat at the gaming table in the notorious bar-come-gambling-den known as Lust. He was surrounded by a dubious ensemble of poker-faced ne're-do-wells and he fitted in seamlessly. Treelo was equally as suspect a character as the next player. He knew he had this game in the palm of his hand. Un'bek had always been his 'A' game and tonight would be no exception. In the palm of the aforementioned hand, he held his insurance policy. A concealed gravity emitter, just in case the tokens didn't go his way. It was a win-win kind of night. The thick haze of narcotic smoke and sleazy grind of discordant 'music' were a dead giveaway as to what kind of place Lust was: not to mention the aroma of Reed Spores mixed with the sweet and sour odour of spilled Raktee and Spice Wine.

The current hand had been playing for at least an hour and Treelo's patience was wearing thin. Kan Vok Tah threw away a malnarch. *He must have the perfect hand to throw away a token of that value,* thought Treelo. To add insult to injury, he also raised the stakes.

"Three hundred thousand credits. Play or fold?" He regarded Treelo with vicious eyes, full of suspicion, and a thinly-veiled urge to inflict pain on him. It was Treelo's lay. He held his tokens casually in his left hand.

"Play". He spoke with a deliberate touch of arrogance and moved to lay his tokens. "Un" then paused for an uncomfortable second or two. The other players stared in anticipation.

"Bek?" One of Kan Vok's men finished the word. Treelo feigned confusion, then repeated.

"Un," and paused again. This time he held Kan Vok's gaze and gave half a wry smile.

"You dare taunt me?!" Kan Vok grew angrier by the second. He stood and slammed his fists on the table, flanked by his henchmen, who reached for their blasters.

"Un'lucky!" laughed Treelo, as he activated the gravity emitter and slapped it onto the gaming table. The device rooted his opponents to the spot.

"I don't tolerate cheats!" Treelo smiled as he scooped up the credits, "Unless that cheat is me." He took a moment to admire his handy work, looked Kan Vok dead in the eye, and said,

"Here, treat yourself to something nice." He threw a solitary credit on to the table and quipped, "You look ridiculous." As he turned to walk away, he laughed to himself and gave a cocky grin. Treelo swaggered out of the gambling house, settled his bill, and left a hefty tip with the attractive young bar keep as he went. Once he was outside, he dropped the nonchalant facade and ran like his life depended on it, and the truth was, it did. Kan Vok Tah was a notorious criminal, and even if Treelo had beaten him fair and square, he would've sent his thugs to retrieve what he had lost, leaving Treelo badly beaten, if not dead. Treelo would need to lay low until he could find transport off Sin. He bargained that the tip he'd left at the bar would go some way to buying him time to find a place to hide.

Back at the gaming table, the gravity emitter's charge was spent and its effects had worn off. Kan Vok Tah smashed the table to splinters with his bare hands.

"Find that arrogant piece of kl'aat dung!" he boomed. "No one tries to make a fool of Kan Vok Tah in his own house." His two thugs charged to the door, and the bar keep misdirected them as they went. Loyalty was hard to come by here, even from your own employees, yet as Treelo had just proved - it was very easily bought. Kan Vok Tah picked up the credit Treelo had thrown to him from the wreckage of the gaming table.

"Big mistake," he spoke in a deep whisper, staring at the credit with a seething anger that looked capable of melting it.

Chapter 4 - Hope

Neela was working the bar. She had watched on keenly as events unfolded at the gaming table. Neela was born on the asteroid, and would tell anyone who bothered to ask her that when she came of age, she just slipped into the family business. The truth however was so much worse. Her Mother had traded her for her own freedom. It was all done by design, from the moment her Mother had decided to get 'accidentally pregnant.' This had been her plan. Neela belonged to Kan Vok Tah, and was doomed from birth to take her Mother's place in the pleasure suites. Neela hadn't let this break her. She believed there was something more, something better for her, and when the chance came she would grab it with both hands and never let go. The stranger who had just played and ultimately humiliated Kan Vok Tah at his gaming table, could be that chance. After the stranger had given her that very generous tip and exited the bar, Neela had misdirected Kan Vok's thugs that gave chase, and now after slipping out of Lust herself, she was on the stranger's tail. He could be the missing piece in Tam's plans and their ticket out of here.

Neela walked the dingy, stone-littered streets in purposeful strides, negotiating the uneven surface of the asteroid's terrain as she hurried along her way. No actual pathways had ever been laid here, and all the litter and debris of the entire asteroid congregated in this area, carried on the pseudo breeze that the atmospheric regulators produced. She shielded her face with her scarf to dull the putrid stench that hung in the air, and it also provided a disguise. Kan Vok's spies were everywhere and she couldn't run the risk of being recognised. Neela tried her best to avoid the gaze of the Peddlers, Reed Dealers and Chokers she encountered with every step. The street people that peppered the darkest nooks of the sector were vicious and desperate. They would mug you if you made eye contact. To look was to buy, and if you didn't pay up, your lot was done. Memories of the time she looked at a Gantuan street child in the wrong way came to mind. She still sported the bite-shaped scars on her right wrist. The stranger really had picked the most unpredictable and desperate part of the asteroid to flee to. The air was warm and greasy here, and the light was so poor that a person could hardly see two metres ahead. The only actual light sources were the dim, trash can fires of the street people, and the glow that emitted from the stars that filled the space above the asteroid's life support dome. Though the sky did go largely unnoticed here, most people tended not to look up. It was an agoraphobia-inducing experience, and an unnerving reminder of how fragile and precarious a place the asteroid was to exist.

Neela was beginning to lose hope, when suddenly she felt an arm around her neck. Someone had grabbed her from behind, and dragged her backwards on her heels across the rough terrain into a shadowy alcove.

"Shhhhh, it's me. There's someone following you." The raspy, whispering voice was familiar. Her abductor removed his hand which had been clamped over her mouth. Neela's heart thumped erratically in her chest.

"Tam! What the hell are you doing here? You nearly scared me to death."

"I could ask you the same question, you nearly worried me to death too. Do you know what hour it is?" Their exchange was cut short by the hiss, crackle and glow of an energy blade igniting. The glow of the blade lit up the shadowy alcove with a shaky blueish hue. It was the stranger from the gambling den. The unstable blue light threw odd shadows about his angular features.

"Why were you following me? Wasn't the tip I left you enough? Thought you'd snatch some more credits for yourself huh?"

"I...." Tam cut Neela's sentence short.

"You were following her!" He drew his blaster from under his robe as he spoke.

"And you, whoever you are, are a terrible hero. This has to be the worst rescue attempt I've ever seen... and put that *'thing'* away." Treelo waved his hand toward Tam's blaster dismissively, as if waving away an annoying bug. "You don't want to attract attention by firing it in a place like this."

"I'd happily take that risk to keep Neela safe."

"Quiet," said Neela in a hushed tone. "Listen."

The sound of shouting and jeering rose in the filthy streets. Kan Vok's thugs were moving through the sector, trying to intimidate information out of the street peddlers and beggars.

"So, what's your play now hero?" said Treelo.

"We don't need a play, it's you they're looking for. Kan Vok will just assume I finished my shift and left. Better still, I could just call them over and reap the rewards for tracking you down. So, I guess the real question here is.. what's your play?" Neela smiled with equal lashings of sarcasm.

"Okay, what do you want? No decent being makes a threat like that unless they want something badly."

"I imagine that we want the same thing as you.... to get off this hellish rock," said Neela.

"That's a fair assumption, but first we need to get out of this sector. Do you two have somewhere safe we could go?"

"We do, but how can we trust you to help us once we get out of here?" Tam was understandably suspicious of Treelo.

"Because...I'm about to save us all," he smiled arrogantly. "Get ready to lead the way when I give the say so." Treelo fumbled in his deep pockets.

"What are you going to do?" Neela wasn't sure that this was going to end well.

"Don't worry, I've got it all under control," said Treelo. He took a blaster charger from his pocket and set it to overload.

"See, we dubious types call this a pauper grenade." The charger began to flash red and Treelo launched it into the street towards the direction of Kan Vok's thugs and the unruly crowds. The charger clattered across the rocky floor, Treelo stepped out of the alcove confidently and ...nothing, except two vicious looking thugs who had just spotted their target.

"Crap," seethed Treelo. One of the thugs, a thick set Zaxvay, with puffy bee-stung features, stooped to pick up the pauper grenade. He looked at Treelo and let out a chesty laugh.
BOOOOOOOM!!!!! The charger went off in his hand; it reduced him to nothing more than a chunky, gore-filled puddle of blood. The remaining thug had been thrown to the floor by the blast. He knew the tables had turned. Moments before, his eyes had been so full of

malice... now they filled with fear and panic as the baying crowd closed in. They set upon him like a pack of crazed animals, kicking and gouging at him, beating him with any heavy objects they could grab.

"RUN!!" yelled Treelo. Tam and Neela ran for their lives, weaving their way through the gloomy darkness of the backstreets. Treelo gave chase, and the three of them disappeared into the twisted alleyways.

Chapter 5 - The Foretelling

The clinical, bright, white walls of Injis's council chamber ricocheted the clean echoing clicks of her heels as they struck the pristine, polished floor. The crowd waited in silent anticipation. She strode effortlessly up a slight incline at the front of the room which represented a stage of sorts and instantly addressed the gathered. No introduction, pomp or ceremony.

"It has been foretold that I, and only I, can lead you to the future you deserve - this prophecy is true. However, it has also been said that I have defied my people's calling and turned my back on healing: this is a lie, I simply see the bigger picture. I may not heal individuals in the archaic way of my ancestors, but this is a new age and new approaches are needed. Planet by planet, galaxy by galaxy, I will heal the entire universe. I will start with the galaxy where it all began, it seems only fitting would you not agree?" Her final question was clearly rhetorical, Injis had no interest in the opinions of lower life forms.

"What about the Protector Droids?" A small voice rose in the otherwise silent room. The voice belonged to Shrimp, a young Scavenger boy who had been orphaned by the frozen sleep of the Zeta Belt. His parents never woke from their frozen slumber. The only clear memories he had of them were the stories they had told him of the indestructible Protector Droids, who had facilitated their imprisonment. In his youthful naivety, Shrimp had blurted out his question. He had always been the type of child to speak before engaging any rational thought processes. The Scavenger Elders had told him long ago, before the frozen sleep, that he had no filter and needed to work on that. Now, in this moment of silent terror, he really wished that he had taken their advice.

"Whoever it was that asked that question, come here to me." The crowd parted, and Shrimp approached Injis with tentative steps.

"There's no need to fear, come closer." The boy knelt before her.

"Please repeat your question child, and I will try my very best to give you an honest answer."

"W, w, what of the Protector Droids?" stuttered Shrimp.
Injis smiled down upon him, his eyes were welled with tears and his voice so full of innocence and curiosity. He wavered with a nervous tremor. Injis placed her hand over his head and the mark of the flame on his neck

burned vivid cyan-blue for all to see. She moved her arm upwards, levitating the boy beneath it. His feet rose above the ground in painful slow motion. Then, without physically touching him, she turned him around to face the crowd. The boy's eyes were filled with Injis's cyan fire and his grubby cheeks were streaked with tears. He was helpless... nothing but a marionette dangling on fragile strings.

"Now child, tell them, tell them all what you see."

"The end."

"And how does this end come to be child?"

"You… you will reunite the White Rock with the Flame of Mora, and The Order of the White Rock shall be born. They will bring victory under your command, and you will rule this galaxy and many more... then the entire universe."

"And what of the Protector Droids you so fear?"

"Gone... devoured by The Hunger."

"And you, what will you do now?"

"I will die for doubting you, it is what I deserve."

"I forgive you child, and now I heal you." Injis inhaled deeply and clenched her fist over Shrimp's head. He burst into cyan flames, which engulfed his entire being. Injis held him under her control for a few more seconds, then splayed her fingers, which released his charred body. The flames had reduced him to a white chalky husk, which disintegrated on contact with the ground. The crowd gasped in unison, as if sucking all oxygen from the room; the collective gasp was followed by a horrified hush which fell over the gathered.

"So, now that you have heard first-hand the fate that will befall Unity's only 'defence', the obsolete Protector Droids, does anyone else have any questions?"
The entire gathering dropped to one knee and bowed their heads in fear and obedience. All except for one, Kalto, Shrimp's loyal friend. He feigned his way through the motions that Injis demanded. But in his mind, the one place that Injis couldn't see, he made a silent vow... a vow to find a way to avenge the murder of his friend.

Chapter 6 - Escape

Tam stopped running, his lungs were fit to burst. Sweat poured from the tips of his nose and chin.

"Through here," said Neela. Tam was too breathless to speak, but managed to gesture to a drain cover - at the foot of the rusted bars that secured the perimeter of the abandoned warehouse.

"What is this dump?"

"This is my home," Tam gasped. "We are just outside the Habitation Dome and this 'dump,' as you so rudely call it, provides me with clean air and water."

"It's also the sanctuary that could save your life, so show some respect," snapped Neela.

"Okay, no offence meant." Once they were inside the warehouse, and after a collective sigh of relief, the interrogation began.

"Why are you here on Sin?" asked Tam.

"Obviously for a quick cash fix," Neela chimed in.

"Hey! Don't speak for me. To be fair though, you are right. I like to think of myself as a liberator of wealth. I steal from the rich and corrupt to give to the poor. Only in this instance the poor is me."

"So apparently charity does indeed begin at home," scoffed Neela. She shook her head disapprovingly.

"Well that's me. So, what's your story Neela?"

"Simple. I was born into the family business and I want out."

"What? That's it?"

"Yes, that's it."

"How about you Hero?"

"I'm not a hero, my name is Tam, and I am the supposed saviour of my species."

"Wow, from one extreme to another," laughed Treelo.

"You haven't even scratched the surface yet," quipped Neela.

"Well, come on then, don't leave me hanging."

"Go on Tam, tell him, he might be able to help. That's the whole reason I started following him in the first place."

"I knew it," snapped Treelo, "I told you Hero, *she* was following *me*."

"What is your name anyways?" asked Tam.

"Treelo.".

"Okay Treelo, try to pay attention to what I am about to tell you. I am Tam Garrel of Veela VI and I carry the Genesis Sphere. The key to my people's legacy."

"Wait a minute, what do you mean carry?"

"I carry the Genesis Sphere within my body."

"So... you're pregnant?"

"No! Well technically yes. But no, it's complicated."

"Well, enlighten me." Treelo forced back a laugh.

"I carry a living sphere which contains the genetic codes of my entire race and the historical records of my planet, and yes, it is sustained inside my body as an infant would be."

"So you're a walking placenta?"

"You're quite the charmer aren't you," snapped Neela. She rolled her eyes.

"Yes an ignorant Kl'aat prong could put it like that. It's a little more sophisticated though. My body is like an incubator, my DNA sustains the sphere. The sphere must be returned to Veela VI and placed in the Cradle of Life, in the heart of the Monl'al mountain range. The Cradle will sustain the sphere and preserve our history for eons to come. Should any Veel'aans have survived in other parts of the galaxy, the sphere will provide them with the tools they need to rebuild our species."

"...And I thought I had problems," laughed Treelo, unable to comprehend the gravity of Tam's situation.

"This isn't funny," snapped Neela, "You clearly don't realise who you've meddled with. Pulling that stunt on Kan Vok Tah was a bad life choice, and now you need to get off this rock as desperately as we do."

"Sorry kids, but I work alone."

"Not anymore you don't. You have the funds, and Tam knows a ship that we could maybe hopefully buy safe passage on."

"Why should I help you and your pregnant boyfriend?"

"Is your memory really that short? I could still turn you in to Kan Vok. Like I said before, Tam knows a ship that can get us away from here."

"Fine, tell me your plan."

"We can lay low here", said Tam. "No one comes out to this part of the asteroid anymore. The Gift Horse is due to dock tomorrow and they never stay for more than one night. We need to intercept Kraddich, he's the captain at the docking bay, and buy our way on to that ship."

"Being who you are, you'll need a disguise. Neela, you're too recognisable from Kan Vok's place and Tam - because you're a Veel'aan. That makes you a collectible rarity in some circles."

"Don't you think he knows that? He only ever goes out after dark in hooded garments, and only then if it's completely necessary."

"Both of you be quiet and listen. I have an idea," said Tam.

Chapter 7 - The Gift Horse

Sin's docking area left a lot to be desired, but people didn't come to a place like this for the scenery. Reed Dealers populated every shady alcove of the area. They gave away samples of the thin, aromatic, tube-like substance to naive newcomers. However, they neglected to tell them how the narcotic spores would literally get their claws into them, causing agonising pain, until more was inhaled to appease the spores that lined the throats of even first-time users. To feed their need was the only way to relax the spores' talons. Droves of Chokers waited in line for their next fix, some sported more than one tracheotomy to achieve maximum intake. The asteroid had no form of policing; just gangster cartels who encouraged the dealers, so long as they got a cut of the profits. Moral pleasantries had no place here, so when Treelo spotted his target, he closed in immediately.

"Captain Kraddich."

"Aye, that I am, what's it to you?"

"Do you have a minute for a mutually beneficial conversation?"

"Beneficial is always a tempting term. But I'm a bit long in the tooth to be falling for the old reed scam."

"Okay, give me some credit, I'm no Reed Dealer. From one scoundrel to another - I need your help, and that help will be reimbursed with a very lucrative return."

"I'm on the hook lad, reel me in."

"What is your rate for safe passage, no questions asked?"

"Two hundred credits per passenger, per day."

"Sounds fair, but I'll give you three hundred."

"Why?"

"We need transport and your guaranteed discretion... badly."

"Where is it you need to be going mate?"

"I'd prefer to tell you that once we are off this dump."

"That works for me. Where be your fellow passengers?"

"No questions asked, yes?"

"None, you have my word."

Treelo beckoned toward a shadowy passageway by a dingy dockside bar. Tam and Neela emerged, clad in full-faced hooded cloaks. Treelo was about to usher them aboard, when Kraddich stepped forward and placed his arm across Tam's chest.

"We agreed four hundred credits per

passenger, yes? Seeing as my discretion means
so much to you." Treelo struggled to hold back
his anger but reluctantly agreed,

"Yes, four hundred."

"This must be some very important cargo. I
didn't know smuggling monks was a thing."
Kraddich laughed, and rubbed his weathered old
hands together.

"Luckily for you, it is," Treelo seethed
through gritted teeth, "Crook."

"Make yourselves comfortable." Kraddich
gestured for them to board the ship, and gave
a nod to the crewman who had been observing
from the entrance. "We set sail at 05:00. I'll
be going about my business now, which
incidentally is none of yours. Works both ways
you see."

They boarded the Gift Horse. Treelo lead the
way, Tam and Neela followed clutching each
other's hands. They were filled with a heady
cocktail of fear, anticipation and nervous
energy.

"You can thank me later," said Treelo, as
he glanced smugly over his shoulder.

Chapter 8 – Wild Space

Wild Space: One week before the activation of The Unity Spire.

Neela woke Tam in a panic. Up until this point, everything had been going smoothly. They'd bid a not so fond farewell to Sin, and watched with not an ounce of sadness as it receded and blended in with the blackness of space. They felt liberated and full of the alien feeling of hope.

   "It's funny, it looks so harmless and unremarkable from here." Neela spoke of the black grey blob that was Sin as it faded out of sight. Gift Horse had passed through the Yetu regions but not in the direction that had been anticipated. The ship passed beyond the Zeta Belt and had entered Wild Space. They had left their own galaxy, and were moving ever further away from anything that was familiar. They had entered a vast expanse of gaseous cloud. A myriad of vivid colours swirled around the Gift Horse, separating, then colliding and intertwining in the ship's wake.

It was so spellbindingly hypnotic to behold that you could almost forget the potential horrors that lurked deeper within Wild Space.

"Treelo," Tam spoke in a loud whisper, and shook him by the arm, "Wake up." Treelo jolted awake and grabbed for his blaster.

"Hey, hey, take it easy. We just thought you should know, we've left our Galaxy."

"What the hell!" snapped Treelo, as he caught sight of the view outside.

"That maniac! We're in Wild Space." He jumped up and ran out of the room. Treelo stormed into Kraddich's quarters, catching him off guard.

"Kraddich! Where the hell are we going?" Kraddich paused the recorded communique he was engrossed in and glared at Treelo.

"As you be here, let me show you something, but first." He looked past Treelo to a crewman who had appeared in the doorway. "Fetch the Monks, I feel a confessional coming on."

* * * * * * * * * * * * * * *

"What is actually going on?" asked Neela, her voice faltered with panic. She and Tam had been unmasked and marched to Kraddich's quarters by two heavy set crewmen.

"All will be revealed Neela."

"How do you know my name?"

"Sssssh, all will become clear," Kraddich spoke with menace, his withered finger with its long grubby nail pressed tight to his lips, which wore a crooked grin. That same finger then tapped on his console to resume playback on the communique. What the visual display showed next made them all sick to the stomach. There was a humanoid being laid on a surgical table. A vial of what appeared to be Micro Droids, had been set free on his naked body. They were like an army of ants with tiny scalpels for legs. They marched perfectly in formation, up and down the test subject's spine, then spread across the entire surface of his skin. Rather than being able to see the actual droids, what they witnessed was the damage they left, as they moved across that poor souls' skin. Waves of crimson washed over him, replacing his natural skin colour as the droids continued to march in formation. His screams couldn't be heard through the transparent box he was trapped in, but they could see the agony on the victim's face. His mouth was shaped in a silent scream, eyes wide in fear, as he wrestled against the restraints that bound him tight to the highly-polished metal table. The scene was cruel and barbaric. The camera angle drew out revealing a being, a species none of them had never seen before. The being began to speak

"I am not beyond compassion. I am merely selective about when I exercise it. Loyalty above all else earns my compassion. Continue to serve me well Kraddich and you need not be concerned with what I have just shown you. Betray me, and you'll get a personal tour of my agony chambers." She spoke in velvet tones;

cyan-blue fire crackled beneath her shell-like white skin. A skin that moved endlessly, cracking and re-joining, to maintain her humanoid form and contain the fire within. What a perfect humanoid form it was too, pert porcelain breasts and sensual curvaceous hips. In a perverse way, she oozed effortless seduction.

"Who, or actually *what* is she?" asked Treelo, shaken, but clearly intrigued by the alluring alien.

"She is Injis, and as you have seen, she deals in physical torment. She says she knows that an end is coming for our galaxy, a time of great change. Her army lies in wait in Wild Space... biding their time, poised and ready to attack when this "end" begins. She will take advantage of the chaos that will follow and bring her own brand of order to the galaxy, and I for one want to make sure that I'm on her good side. As she just said, she can 'show compassion,' and I mean to earn some. That's why we're taking this slight detour into Wild Space, to collect her cargo and transport it to Exhilar.

"Why Exhilar?" asked Treelo "It's a holiday resort, and she doesn't look like a tourist."

"Injis needs something that she says only she can find there."

"Why explain all of this to us?" gulped Treelo.

"Well here's the thing," sighed Kraddich, "I'm only sharing this with you - firstly because you barged in so rudely whilst I was watching it, and secondly, sadly…" He exhaled at length and sighed, "I'll be needing to kill you."

"What? Why would you want to kill me?" stuttered Treelo.

"Now now, it's rude to answer a question with a question. There's a little something you forgot to tell old Kraddich, isn't there?"

"Look, we just wanted to get off that forsaken rock, to make a better life, and you said no questions." Treelo had lost his facade of calm level-headedness; being told you are about to be killed in unfamiliar space will do that to a person.

"True enough, I don't usually ask questions of my paying passengers, but you three are wanted by Kan Vok Tah. That's not okay, and now that you've seen who i'm transporting for, it's even less so."

"Come on! We didn't ask to see that, we're not gonna say anything, and besides, people would think we were nuts, telling a story like that. It's not like we haven't paid way over the odds for safe passage. Give us a break. What do you want? More credits? Kraddich please, we wouldn't say a word to Kan Vok, and who would believe us about the blue and white fire woman? No one that's who. See... I already forgot her name," Treelo blurted out the mess of words, struggling to form coherent sentences.

"Credits won't save my hide if Kan Vok Tah finds out I helped you. He's also put a bounty on your heads that adds up to much more than the fee I'm charging you. I'll be needing something truly spectacular to keep me from taking all of your credits and handing you back to the man himself."

"Don't be hasty. How about this?" Treelo paused and glanced knowingly at Tam and Neela, then he continued to speak,

"Kraddich. I respect you and I believe you are a man of very good judgement." There it was, the nonchalant swagger had returned. "I'll wager that my good friend Tam here can offer you something beyond your most unreachable imaginings."

"Or I could just sell him into slavery. A rarity such as he, a Veel'aan, would fetch a handsome price on the dark markets." Greed burned in the withered, old, space pirate's eyes, underlined by his vicious slit of a grin.

"But he can offer you more than money. Money runs out. I've seen pirate's spending habits and believe me, it would run out fast. What he can offer you is something truly remarkable."

"Go on, this should be good," said Kraddich, mockingly.

"He can give you a world of your very own, to do with as you please. You could be the ruler of your own planet, and all its riches would belong to you. Everything that lay upon

and beneath its surface. As you're on the blue
fire lady's good side, she would surely leave
you to go about your kingly business, as a
reward for your loyal services."
Treelo was playing Kraddich, he needed to save
his skin, and this way he could get Tam to
where he needed to go, or at least that's what
he had convinced himself he was doing.

   "Is this true boy?"

   "Yes, I am the last of my people. As sole
heir to Veela VI, my home planet is now mine
to do with as I see fit."

   "And you would give such a prize to a
scoundrel such as old Kraddich?"

   "I have no love for that planet. I was
sacrificed and abandoned to protect it's
pathetic history. If it means saving Neela's
life, then it is yours."

   "Huh hmm," Treelo interrupted.

   "And Treelo's life of course."

   "Then this is your lucky day. I do believe
we have an accord." Kraddich spat in the palm
of his hand and offered it to Tam.

   "Thanks, but you have my word and I hope
that is enough," he grimaced.

   "Suit yerself boy, pleasure doing business
with ya. But be warned. If you're lying to me,
things are gonna get pretty bad and pretty
damn fast for all of you." Kraddich tapped his
sheathed blade. "Once I have completed my
business here, you can take me to my new
planet, gonna have to change that name
though."
He walked away, whistling an off-key tune to

himself, his classic greedy smile all too
evident.

Tam had never wanted to be the saviour of his
people's legacy, but in that moment, he
realised that he did care. He was proud of who
his people had been before their cowardly
demise, a fact that his frustration at his
hopeless plight had blinded him to. The doubts
he'd had - melted away. It hadn't occurred to
him that, up until this point, he had been in
total denial, too afraid to care. It had
seemed an impossible task, but now he had a
chance to actually fulfil his mission. The
hardship he had endured may not have been for
nothing after all. For now, he would play this
game as a means to an end, and how he got his
planet back would be down to Treelo.

    "Treelo, you better have a plan," seethed
Neela.

    "No sweat, I'm a winging it type. I do my
best work under pressure."

    "Here's some pressure for you. As you just
left me no choice but to gift my planet to
pirates, how do you plan to stop them from
actually claiming it, so I can complete my
mission?"

    "Take it easy, I'll think of something.
Besides, I've just got you a ride to where you
need to go, and not to mention saved all of
our arses. A thank you would be nice." He
turned away from them, and had a muted
conversation with himself. "Thanks for saving
our lives Treelo. Yay what a guy. No, no it

was nothing really, you're welcome."

Chapter 9 - Veela VI

"There she is, in all her shining glory," sighed Tam. He knew his homecoming would be bittersweet, but it had been completely ruined by the predicament Treelo had put them in.

"Ahhhh, she is a beauty." Kraddich rubbed his grubby little hands together,

"So, boy, do we sign deeds or what?"

"I need to go to the surface to prepare for your arrival. I need Neela and Treelo with me to make the correct preparations. Don't worry, we are happy to take a security detail of your choosing with us," Tam lied, convincingly.

"Good, because you'd be going nowhere without one," cackled Kraddich, with his slit-like mouth. "Ruindor, take our friends to Lander Three, Mansk will be your pilot. I'll be sure he's onboard, waiting for when you get there....and Ruindor, watch that one, he's slippery." Kraddich was gesturing to Treelo.

"Hey, why just me?" he protested.

"We'll make contact when the appropriate preparations have been made," said Tam.

"Make it quick. I grow impatient, now I have me eyes on me prize." Within minutes, the lander was away on a course to the Rooktrowe region, on the far side of Veela VI.

* * * * * * * * * * * * * * * *

A lone battle yacht emerged from the cover of Veela's twin moons. It was a bizarre vessel; a hybrid pleasure cruiser of sleek, luxurious design, fitted with the heavy artillery and armour of a destroyer. Although there could be no doubt what the ship's purpose was on this day. Cannons and missile turrets littered its decks. The nose section of the vessel had been fitted with an ancient battering ram. An antiquated slab of solid metal and spikes, it was an intimidating sight from a barbaric time that promised to deliver devastating brutality. The ship had locked on to its prey and wasted no time in launching its assault.

"Captain! We have incoming." The hybrid ship's weapons array lit up - unleashing intense fire and fury upon the Gift Horse.

"Return fire!!" shouted Kraddich. Even though he was clearly outgunned, Kraddich's philosophy remained: fight fire with fire. A barrage of pulse blasts thumped into the flank of the Gift Horse, swiftly followed by armour piercing missiles that penetrated the ship's recovering shields. Chunks of ancient, splintered wood were blasted from the reinforced metal fuselage of Kraddich's ship.

Oxygen hissed from the multiple breach points that peppered the doomed ship's twisted metal infrastructure.

****

The Lander's proximity sensors chimed, but their tones were drowned out by the sound of debris clattering against the aft shields. Mansk swept the Lander in a one-eighty. The view screen exploded with images of blazing fire and the flashes of imploding shields and power cells. The shocking image of the Gift Horse being decimated threw Mansk and Ruindor into total shock. They stared, open-mouthed, at the horror that unfolded before them, which completely undermined their facade of menacing fearlessness. Neela seized the opportunity; she snatched Ruindor's blaster from his holster, and without hesitation, she ended both guards with a pair of swift headshots.

"Yes Neela! See, what did I tell you?" laughed Treelo.

"Everything always works out in the end." He spoke as if this was his plan all along.

"Shut up Treelo and take the controls," barked Neela, "And get us out of here now!" She was visibly shaken. Tam couldn't speak, he was both grateful and horrified. He never imagined his sweet Neela could be so brutal and cold- blooded.

The hybrid ship's battering ram pummeled its way through the Gift Horse, reducing her to shrapnel and kindling. The savage vessel emerged through the wreckage like a monstrous dragon rising through a sea of hellfire, it's terrifying silhouette backlit by the flame and chaos of the wrecked vessel that was the Gift Horse. It conjured the image of a descending dragon, coming to claim their souls.

"You were saying Treelo?" Neela had regained enough composure to aim barbed comments at Treelo once more. "That's The Spectre, Kan Vok Tah's battlecruiser."

"There's no time for I told you so Neela, we need to get out of here now." Treelo pushed the lander as hard as it would go, but it was a futile exercise. The Spectre was gaining on them easily, it's docking clamps were open, poised ready to ensnare them. Treelo twisted and turned the lander, exhausting his complete repertoire of evasive manoeuvres, but it was no use. With a menacingly heavy *thunk*, the docking clamps had secured a clean magnalock onto the Lander. Tam remained silent, disorientated, and out of his depth. He had never witnessed violence of this magnitude, especially from someone he loved.

The boarding hatch hissed open. Kan Vok Tah and two of his men stepped heavily onto the lander.

"At least you've saved me one job," he said - eyeing the slain bodies of Ruindor and Mansk. He nodded towards Treelo and Tam, and his thugs secured them both at blasterpoint. Kan Vok Tah rolled a credit between his fat fingers, like an amateur magician. The same credit that Treelo had tossed to him at the gaming table back on Sin.

"You!" he addressed Treelo, "You dared to come into my house and cheat me at my own gaming table! That took some gargantuan balls and honestly, I admire your audacity. In another life we could have been allies, friends even. You, my would-be-friend, can consider yourself fortunate on this occasion. You stole my money, but money isn't everything. Another member of your rebellious little trio has done me a far more unforgivable wrong." Kan Vok stomped over to Neela and sighed, his sour breath invaded her nostrils. He traced an invisible line down her cheek and across her throat with his finger. Neela recoiled, his grubby hand wreaked of stale sweat and used credits.

"You Neela are my property, and you have betrayed me. Did you really think I would just let you go?"

"You're right, I have betrayed you, and I'd do it again in a heartbeat. You disgust me. Every time you ever touched me my skin crawled, and I had to force back the sickness that rose in my throat."

"Ahhhhh, such fight, that's why you were always my favourite toy. I was even willing to offer you one more chance to return to Sin with me."

"Never! I would rather die."

"Neela, NO!" Tam shouted. The muscle-bound thug that guarded him delivered a solid blow to the small of his back, with the butt of his blaster. The force of the blow knocked the air clean out of his lungs.

"Tut, tut, tut, such a waste," said Kan Vok, who shook his fat head. He flipped the credit at Tam, "Here boy, bury her somewhere nice. If you make it out of this bucket-of-bolts alive." Neela stood defiant, without so much as a flicker of emotion. With a single fluid movement Kan Vok drew a small, but lethal, blade from his belt and slit her throat.

"No!" screamed Tam, he could only watch helplessly as Neela's body slammed onto the grilled metal floor of the lander. Kan Vok gave a throaty laugh, then cleaned Neela's blood from his blade with his vulgar swollen tongue. Without so much as a blink, he turned his attention towards Treelo.

"Where are my manners? In all the excitement, I almost forgot about you." He drew his blaster and casually delivered a bolt to Treelo's gut. Treelo moaned through gritted teeth, but he would not give Kan Vok the pleasure of his screams.

"That shot right there, my would-be-friend, will kill you. When? Well your guess is as good as mine. So... who looks ridiculous now?" Kan Vok's thugs exited the lander, laughing cruelly. Kan Vok backed out behind them. He looked around the lander, which he had reduced to a blood-drenched murder scene, and closed the boarding hatch. He cruelly smiled and waved playfully through the plexiglass, in the manner you would wave to a small child. With a hiss of pressurised air, he jettisoned the lander from his docking clamps.

"Help me," Treelo shouted at Tam in panic, he had to stem the bleeding. Tam was completely unresponsive. There was only one option, Treelo had to stop the bleeding himself. He removed the concealed energy blade that he had smuggled in his boot, and thrust it into the blaster wound. He screamed out in agony as he activated the blade, drowning out it's static crackle and the sizzle of burning flesh. The wound was cauterized, but the searing pain was excruciating, and it was too much for his body to take... he passed out cold. On the opposite side of the lander, Tam sat frozen in silent, unblinking shock. His mind couldn't process or rationalise any of what had just transpired. He was physically and mentally numb.

Chapter 10 - Left For Dead

Tam wasn't sure how much time had passed since they had been set adrift. What he did know was that he must be hallucinating. A voice had been talking to him, urging him to kill Treelo. The voice was Neela's, but he knew that was impossible. Her cold, slaughtered body still layed in a pool of her own coagulated blood in front of him. *'Kill him, if you ever truly loved me you'd do it.'* Tam clamped his hands over his ears and squeezed his eyes shut. *'It's his fault I'm dead, his plan is what led us here, KILL HIM!'* Neela's voice was tormenting him, urging him to do the unspeakable.

"NO!" screamed Tam.

A blinding flash of light illuminated not just the interior of the lander, but everything outside it too. The flash was accompanied by silence, a beautiful, blissful silence. It felt as if time and motion stood still. The

faux voice of Neela that had tormented Tam's

mind had fallen silent. He peered cautiously out from between his fingers, which had been knitted in front of his eyes - cautious of any additional horrors that may await. An odourless black smoke hung in the silent air, and it weaved around like the tail of a kite on a gentle breeze. The smoke slowly drifted towards Treelo, who had been roused by Tam's screaming. He was awake, but barely hanging on to consciousness. Tam couldn't believe his eyes; the black smoke took solid form and within seconds there were two Treelo's, laying on the floor facing one another. The real Treelo screamed in horror. He was understandably freaked out. The doppelganger before him mimicked his every move, but it did so in deafening silence. It was like it had been set to mute. Its mouth opened and closed, mirroring Treelo's screams and ravings, but still it made no sound. Tam gaped in terror.

"Kill it!" screamed Treelo.

His words jolted Tam into action. He cautiously stooped to pick up Ruindor's blaster from the blood-soaked floor where Neela had dropped it. He held the blaster with both hands, to steady his aim, and unleashed a bolt that barely clipped the doppelganger, but it was enough. White vapour poured from the wound. All colour and detail drained from the doppelganger, leaving a motionless, transparent shell. Treelo kicked out at it, the brittle substance cracked and shattered into fractured pieces. The white vapour that had poured from the shell solidified, and formed a small white rock.

"What on Tah was that thing?"

"I think it was The Hushed."

"The Hushed? You believe in those stories? I always thought they were made up to scare bad kids into behaving," Treelo wheezed.

"No, you're wrong Treelo, they are very real. But this is something I never knew could happen. It was here in our physical realm and I, I mean we killed it. There's only one explanation. Someone, or something, has activated the Unity Spire."

"More kids stories. You are clearly in shock my friend."

"Well how do you explain what just happened?"

"Mass hallucination caused by shared stress and trauma."

"Hallucinations don't leave parts of themselves behind." Tam picked the white rock from the brittle, plastic fragments and held it in front of Treelo.

"None of this really matters Tam, in case you forgot I'm dying, and we're floating miles from anywhere with no supplies, so that means you're pretty much dead too." Tam slumped to the floor next to Neela's lifeless body. He stroked her once beautiful, now blood- matted hair, and began to cry. He caressed her cheek with his fingers; her skin was icy cold to the touch and as white as freshly fallen snow.

"I know," Tam replied, in a completely defeated tone. His vision blurred, and as he slipped from consciousness, he whispered, "My love, I am so sorry I could not protect you. I have failed you and my people." The Genesis Sphere glowed in Tam's stomach, a healing glow that travelled through his entire being. The very thing that he had protected had now become his protector.

Chapter 11 - Gliis

Planet Unity: One day after activation of The Unity Spire.

Gliis woke with an uneasy feeling in his gut. He'd had that same dream again. Smoke turned to stone and an unfamiliar voice whispered.

"Listen and you will hear." That same small white rock now hung on a leather thong around his neck. Gliis had kept it as a trophy. He had plucked it from the battlefield after the victory over The Hushed. He thought it symbolic; he kept the stone captive as The Hushed had kept his Mother Etala Maas and her people captive in the Endless War. Gliis thought of her now as he regarded his face in the mirror. He looked deep into his unmatching eyes, his left eye was the image of his mother's eyes. Its golden yellow iris almost gem-like and subtly metallic. In stark contrast, his right eye was a piercing sapphire blue, like the crystal pools of the planet Home. He forgot from time to time how unique his appearance was. His startling wide eyes looked out from a silken complexion which was ghost-like in its pallor. A shock of unkempt, blue-black hair framed his young face. As he stared intently at his reflection, he wondered what his mother would make of his use of the white rock; a tool that gave him glimpses of what people were thinking and feeling. He was pretty sure that she would approve. He was using it to benefit The Unity, and despite his unnerving recurring dreams, the stone didn't feel in any way dangerous or a threat to him. It was a vastly different sensation to the one he had witnessed Lu endure with the mind invasion of The Hushed, back on Veela VI. This sensation felt pure and untainted. This new sense had also aided him in ascertaining which delegates were true friends of The Unity, with honest intentions, and those who would try to use The Unity to push their own agenda. Gliis had been advising Lu accordingly, never letting on how he knew their intentions. He had an inkling that Lu was beginning to grow suspicious, but he had played it off as his impeccable judge of character.

Chapter 12 - Salvation?

Two days had passed since Lu's broadcast to the people of the galaxy. Many delegates had already arrived. They were buzzing with excitement at the prospect of a new beginning: as an equal part of the new Unity. It wasn't all peace and harmony though. There was still an element of unrest and uncertainty in a few of the more remote regions, and even one or two of the neighbouring ones. Some of the delegations had reported civil war; rising rebellions and crime syndicates jostling for power on their home worlds. While others had told of vast wreckage from what must have been a conflict in Veel'aan space. The debris clearly wasn't the orbiting remnants of the Ferrucian destroyer The Devastator. This was charred, splintered wood and burred metal, tonnes of drifting wreckage. Seventeen and a small crew had been deployed in his repurposed fighter, which had finally been named The Hope. It was a fitting name for any ship in the current climate. The Hope was headed to Veel'aan space to investigate the reported wreckage.

"How exciting, my old compadre. Brothers in arms, hitting the space trail once again," Zero-Nine bellowed, full of enthusiasm.

"And Sisters too of course: Mardran and you Zen, do you mind me calling you Zen? Or do you prefer Dara or Zee?"

"Does hpe ever stop?" smirked Zendara.

"No, unfortunately he does not." Seventeen's displeasure at having Zero-Nine onboard for the mission was abundantly clear for all to see. However, Tecta had insisted. Zero-Nine,(despite his many foibles), was a scanning specialist, and that was exactly what this mission needed.

"Come on Seventeen, this is an adventure. Surely even you, the father of all things miserable, must have missed this."

"This is a mission Zero Nine! Remember that, and stop distracting me." Zendara smirked once again and replied to Zero- Nine in hushed tones,

"Zee sounds good, I like that one."

"Ok Zee," bellowed Zero Nine, in his ever-unsubtle manner, "onward to our destiny!"

"Please don't encourage him Zendara," sniped Seventeen.

Mardran, The Hope's pilot, listened to her crew mate's exchanges with quiet bewilderment. Since the events of the Endless War, Mardran had been a creature of few words, but her keen senses didn't miss a trick.

"Sorry to 'distract' you my Lord and Master, but my scans have picked up a short distance craft. The vessel contains two faint humanoid life signatures." said Zero-Nine.

"Mardran, try hailing them." Seventeen was intentionally ignoring Zero-Nine's comments.

"Their comms are receiving my hail, but they are not responding."

"Keep trying. Zendara, with me, prepare to board the vessel."

"Really?" questioned Zero-Nine, "And what am I supposed to do, sit here and tweak my relays?"

"No, you need to do the one useful thing that you are capable of! Scanning! Advise us of any changes inside the vessel."

"Rude."

"It's okay Zero, you can keep me company," said Mardran.

"I do not need your pity Mardran. I will however gratefully accept it, thank you."

"What is the deal with you two anyway?"

"Me and Zee? Oh, we're just friends for now, but I think we could be more."

"No," laughed Mardran, "You and Seventeen."

"Oh him. He's never liked me. He has no sense of humour."

* * * * * * * * * * * * *

Seventeen and Zendara secured the docking link between The Hope and the lander.

"Zero-Nine - is the atmosphere inside

breathable for Zendara?"

"Affirmative, the air is acceptable, but in short supply. Although you should prepare yourselves for high levels of odour. Physical decay readings are extremely high, and there's plasma, so much spilled plasma." The lander door hissed open. Zendara covered her mouth and nose, the nausea-inducing stench hit her like a rancid tsunami. The interior of the lander resembled the killing floor of an uncleansed abattoir. She tried her best to ignore the scenes of horror and gore that painted the inside of the lander, and set about her tasks. She scanned Treelo who was still, unsurprisingly, unconscious.

"A couple of hours more and this one would be dead. We need to get him to the sick bay. She moved on to Tam. "This one's condition is okay physically, but he's non-responsive. Extended shock syndrome is my best guess at this point."

"Zendara, he is Veel'aan." Seventeen was uncharacteristically stunned.

"Whatever he is, we need to get him and his friend to the sick bay right now."

* * * * * * * * * * *

Within hours, Treelo and Tam were stabilised. Seventeen wasted no time in bringing them up to speed with the current status of the galaxy. He recounted the story of the Unity Spire in possibly a little too much detail.

Tam seethed quietly when he learned Lu had given Veela VI to the R'aal, though he showed no sign of emotion.

"Will she ever be surprised to see you, another Veel'aan?" Zero chipped in.

"After everything I have just heard, I'm very keen to meet her too." Tam gripped Kan Vok's credit tightly in his clenched fist. In his traumatised state, his eyes grew dark; he would deal with him later, but first his thoughts turned to what he would say and how he would punish the great 'hero' Nataalu for her betrayal.

Chapter 13 - Tam Garrel

Planet Unity: Four days after the activation of The Unity Spire.

Seventeen burst through the door and levelled his wrist blasters at Tam. Treelo trailed in behind him, under the close watch of a further Protector Droid.

"I would tell you that you have an intruder, but it appears I am a little late. I apologise, for it is I who brought him here to Unity. I kept his heritage a secret to surprise you Nataalu, once he had recovered."

"We have the situation under control. It's okay Seventeen. However, it is certainly a surprise," said Tecta.

"It's not okay!" screamed Tam, his rage had gotten the better of him, "You warned them I would seek revenge on Nataalu?" He glared psychotically at Treelo, who stepped forward.

"I am sorry Tam, I just didn't want you to do anything you would regret. I had to tell them, you've not been yourself since Nee…."

"Don't even say her name traitor!"

"Tam," said Lu, "That is what you said your name is? I'm listening," spoke Lu, in a soothing tone. "Explain your presence here, and we will listen to what you have to say. Please forgive my staring but I have never seen another Veel'aan before, and until this moment, I honestly believed that I was the last of our kind."

"There's a good reason for that!" spat Tam. He paced the floor furiously, in a state of complete agitation. "There was a plan! Admittedly a plan I was opposed to, but that is something that you, Nataalu, wouldn't know anything about. You were saved and delivered into a life of privilege before the attack on Veela VI was even dreamed of. I'll tell you how I'm still here. I carry the Genesis Sphere: the means to bring our people's legacy back to our home planet."

"The Genesis Sphere? I thought that was a Vee'laan legend." Lu failed to disguise her shock.

"I would've thought that you, who activated the Unity Spire, would have more belief."

"When you say carrying. Does that mean you're pregnant?" said Taire. He looked puzzled, and Gliis even more so.

"Yes! Why not mock and belittle me further with your ignorance. I'm sure the all-knowing Nataalu knows the legend, she can explain it to you. Right now, I need you to listen to me, you are not untouchable, and you are far from the peace you seek. I could've taken you all out at any second had I been so inclined. This isn't about me though. It's about our race and our galaxy." Tecta stiffened and stood.

"You overestimate yourself boy. You would not have lasted a milli-second had you come here with murder in mind."

"You! A so-called Protector Droid would kill me?" He spoke with openly fake surprise. "Of course, you would. Just like you might as well have murdered my people. Explain something to me. Why didn't you protect Veela VI when the Twenty Four-Hour War came? You stood by and did nothing, whilst my people, including my stupid parents, were slaughtered."

"You know nothing of the truth." There was anger in Tecta's voice and it rose in volume.

"Tecta, let him speak," said Lu forcefully.

"Anyway, I digress," laughed Tam, maniacally. He then continued to speak with totally uncharacteristic abandon, completely dismissing Tecta's comments. "If I'm honest, at first I couldn't have cared less about Veela VI. I believed my parents were fools who died a meaningless death, and I was filled with rage and resentment. However, everything paled in insignificance in comparison to what I have seen in the Wild Space beyond our galaxy. There lies a threat, far beyond anything that any of us have ever encountered, and we all need to prepare. I must protect my home world, and will all have to fight for our galaxy. Nothing is quite as sobering as the threat of impending obliteration."

"Have you not heard of our victory over The Hushed?" Tecta spoke in an uncharacteristically boastful manner. Tam's comments about the Twenty Four-Hour War had hurt him, and he was still angered.

"Tecta, please, there will be time to explain all to Tam later. It can wait, he is angry and as you well know, you did nothing wrong. Tam will come to understand this in good time."

"Ah The Hushed, yes, well done you," Tam applauded, mockingly. "Even I killed one of them on the lander where you found us, and I was half dead at the time."

Vrin entered the Siblings' chamber with Greem. The fire crackled and glowed, providing a backdrop of peace and soothing warmth to the frenetic scene. Fortunately the chamber was large enough to accomodate the seemingly endless stream of unexpected guests that now populated it this evening.

"He speaks some truth. The stillness that the galaxy felt when we defeated The Hushed was far too short-lived. I have felt concern and unease. I also sense his honesty and desperation; this boy is telling *his* truth."

"Finally, someone with some sense." Tam panted heavily, sweat poured from his forehead and clammy hands. He had nowhere near recovered from the ordeal on the lander, and his outbursts had agitated his fragile mental and physical states. Vrin had aged at an unnatural rate in the days that had passed since the activation of The Unity Spire. Her physical self looked to have grown younger - but her inner wisdom, theories and feelings were still older and wiser than any of the others gathered here.

"Thank you Vrin," smiled Lu. "Tam, we will discuss what you have told us with the council."

"There's no time for discussion. You have to act now!" Tam snapped.

"We will discuss this with the council before we do anything. However, if you would indulge me, I would like to hear more about you and the events that have led you to be here." Lu spoke gently, attempting to calm Tam's heightened state and bring him back to some semblance of rationality.

"If it helps you decide to do the right thing and act, I will do as you ask."

"It won't do your cause any harm," smiled Lu. "Taire, would you fetch some warm, spiced Raktee for our guest please? I think I could use one too." Taire nodded and left the room.

Gliis had been staring intently at Tam the whole time he had been speaking. The White Rock's effects had allowed him to feel Tam's emotions. He approached Lu and whispered in her ear,

"He is not just angry at you sister, he has lost someone he loved, and his rage is fuelled by that loss. There is much more to him, it may not seem like it now, but he is on our side, the side of peace."

"How do you know this Gliis?"

"I... erm... I just have a feeling."

"Okay," said Lu, her voice and features were laced with suspicion, "We will speak more on this later."

Vrin watched the sibling's whispered exchanges with a questioning curiosity.

* * * * * * * * * * * *

Nataalu asked everyone, with the exception of Tecta and Tam, to leave the room. Tam eyed Tecta suspiciously.

"Maybe you should begin Tecta; try to put Tam's mind at ease." Tecta explained why the Protector Droids could not intervene in the Twenty Four-Hour War, and how it was over before they had even received word that it had started. In any case, the Veel'aans had given the Royals previous instructions. They had expressly asked them not to intervene in any conflict on Veela VI, (and The Royals being the sticklers that they were), followed this request to the letter. It was like a planetary DNR. Tam's people had decided martyrdom was the route that they needed to take to achieve their end goal: the rebirth of Veela VI, to deny the Feruccians' their fight, and to stay true to their own beliefs.

"I appreciate you not pulling any punches and telling it straight Tecta." Tam was finding it increasingly difficult to dislike

Lu or Tecta. They felt familiar somehow, but he wasn't quite ready to let go of his rage. He feared it was the only thing that still held him together.

"Tam, whilst we are speaking plainly, I just wanted to say I am so sorry. You were quite right earlier when you said I would know nothing of the plan to save Veela VI, or that the Genesis Sphere was more than a myth. I still have much to learn about our planet. I urge you to understand that the R'aal were homeless, and their intentions pure. I do, however, understand that I have made an unintentional error of judgement in gifting them Veela VI, before I knew all the facts."

"It takes guts to apologise and admit when you made a mistake. Now you just need to make things right. Prove yourself to be the great leader that you have been portrayed as, and give us back our planet, so that I may fulfil my mission. It is my only purpose, and all that I have left." Tam broke down, exhausted from his rage and unfathomable sadness. Taire returned with the Raktee, and set it down on a small table between two high-backed chairs where Lu and Tam sat. Tecta took his leave with Taire.

"I will leave the two of you to speak further. I shall be just outside the door," spoke Tecta, with protective parental suspicion. Lu thanked them both, then turned her full attention back to Tam, who was still sobbing. He started to speak again.

"A new threat rises from Wild Space. She

will come to destroy your new-found Unity while it is still in its infancy, before you have had the chance to grow strong."

"We are strong Tam. We have survived unthinkable horrors in recent days, and we will stop this latest threat." Lu moved closer to Tam. "May I?" She gestured to embrace him, though Tam was too distraught to respond. She wrapped her slender arms around him and pulled him close. Tam reciprocated, clamping his arms tightly around Lu's waist. Her cheek touched his, and in that moment of skin-on-skin contact, something happened that neither of them had expected.

A wave of tingling ecstasy pulsed through their entire beings. They moaned in mutual pleasure, and their pale violet skin transformed to vibrant, pulsating works of art. The Genesis Sphere had connected them in recognition of their Veel'aan heritage. The connection was not just physical. It was spiritual, almost sexual in its intimacy, but it was even more than that. This was a recognition and connecting of two souls. They arched back and regarded each other in wonder, looking deep into each other's violet eyes. Every fibre of their beings had become prickled and hypersensitive. Instinctively, they pressed their foreheads together and their fingers intertwined. The Genesis Sphere enabled them to share their thoughts, feelings and experiences. They looked breathlessly into one another's eyes, and each of their lives flashed through the other's mind, like a movie in hyper fast-forward. Every crystal-clear image was accompanied by the corresponding emotion. They now understood each other intimately - what the others journey had been - and how they had come to be here in this moment. They lay entwined in each other's arms, in the gentle flicker and glow of the fire. They slipped into the most restful sleep that either of them could ever recall.

Chapter 14 - Dreams

Gliis' dream came again, only this time it was
very different. This was pure symbolism. The
White Rock was showing him more. The rock
became white smoke that mixed with black
smoke, then solidified, and once again became
stone. Blue flames began to roar and engulf
the white rock, burning the black smoke out of
it... a thin ribbon of black smoke remained.
It danced in the rhythm of the flames. The
rock pulsed and vibrated, and the flames
roared, dwarfing the black smoke. It appeared
the three colours were fighting for control.
With a deafening crack, the rock exploded and
once again became vapour. The white vapour
began to regroup slowly, forming a new
pristine white rock. A spark of blue ember
came to rest amidst the forming rock; the
ember became pure blue flame. The black smoke
had been defeated, and what remained was the
harmony of the blue and the white.

Gliis snapped awake, clammy and breathless,
clutching the White Rock to his chest. His

head was filled with the voices, thoughts and feelings of the people that populated the rooms and corridors of the palace. He fought to focus his mind, to suppress the sounds and images. A warmth emanated from the rock and penetrated his hands, a soothing warmth that dulled his keen senses. There was no time to dwell on his dream. He and his siblings were due to address the council with Tam shortly. He shook off the last remnants of sleep and readied himself for the meeting.

Chapter 15 - The Mora

Tam set the scene for the impending invasion in graphic detail. He did his best to convey the terror that was Injis. He told of her plans to take control of the galaxy after an 'End' of sorts: her plans to exploit the chaos.

"There has been an end, the end of The Hushed," said Lu.

"And there is a degree of confusion in the galaxy while we all find our place in the new Unity, but I wouldn't call it chaos," said Targole,"I'll wager that she is a scare monger - a would be dictator." Targole's response was intended to play down the threat. He had led his people in the battle for Unity. They had left their home in the silence to fight the good fight with the siblings and he struggled with the notion of another conflict.

"No!" shouted Tam, "She is a real threat."

"I have seen who she is, and her intentions are purely evil," said Lu, who supported Tam.

"She is of a species I have never

encountered," added Treelo, "And I have been to some of the darkest and most remote edges of our galaxy." Tam described Injis's physical appearance in intricate detail.

"This cannot be!" stated Tecta in disbelief, "She is Mora."

"No. Her name Injis, this one say." Pilot pointed at Tam.

"Of The Mora people Pilot," smirked Lu, gesturing for pilot to be quiet. Pilot looked like someone had just turned on a light switch, as his expression changed from puzzled to embarrassment, then returned to his usual toothy grin. His people could lighten any situation, intentionally or otherwise, no matter how grim. Tecta brought the council swiftly back to business.

"The Mora race is older than we Protector Droids, even older than the Core Loway. But The Mora were peaceful healers. They left our Galaxy millennia ago. It was a self-imposed exile, —due to the actions of a single Mora. The details of what happened are vague at best, hidden or believed lost in the passage of time, long before the era of our birth. All that is known is that the guilt was too much to bare, and their entire species left our Galaxy, in search of knowledge to advance their already impressive medical prowess. They vowed never to return until they found a way to make things right, and even prevent death. There is something very, very wrong with this situation. We need to figure out why she has returned, and why she is seemingly acting alone."

"From what we saw, peaceful is far from what Injis was," Treelo chipped in. "She was torturing a test subject and it certainly didn't look like she was trying to heal him. That poor soul was in a whole universe of pain. We were just grateful to get out of there in one piece. Old Kraddich was playing with fire, throwing his lot in with that one."

"Since The Mora locked the flame, all that remains on Pharmora is volcanic wasteland and the White Rocks. What does she want with either of those?" Tecta thought out loud.

"I think I might know," said Gliis tentatively. He opened the neck of his tunic to reveal the White Rock that he wore. The council gasped at the sight of the rock.

"Gliis, why do you keep the remnants of a slayed Hushed?" Lu's voice was full of concern.

"The rock speaks to me in dreams."

"Is he all there?" laughed Treelo, followed by some choice expletives after Pilot had kicked him in the shin and snapped,

"You respect! Friend Gliis, you speak. Pilot listen."

"You will all think that my mind has malfunctioned." Gliis still carried Tecta's inflections in his voice.

"Brother, after what we have seen and been through, I firmly believe that nothing is impossible." Taire placed a reassuring hand on his brother's shoulder.

"The White Rocks, they do talk to me. They

are not evil like The Hushed. They long to be
returned to their planet of origin. The
planet's core calls to them. They have been
abused firstly by The Hushed, but when The
Hushed were destroyed, it set the essence of
the White Rocks free, allowing them to return
to their natural state. They are stranded,
scattered throughout the galaxy. This new
evil... she is planning to claim them for her
own, to abuse them for their power once
again."

"Gliis, is this how you knew about Tam's
intentions?" Lu looked at Tam coyly, the
intimacy that they had shared caused her to
blush faintly.

"Yes, and all the other newcomers to The
Unity, I feel their thoughts and emotions."

Targole stood and spoke with serious intent.
"The properties of these rocks are
incidental Nataalu. Do not prod the sleeping
beast. Let it lie. We must not lower ourselves
to this Injis's level. What she does on that
world does not concern us. If we move against
her supposed threat, we could trigger another
war. What happened to our promise of peace?
Are we to break it because some Alien wants us
to do what... throw rocks at us?"

"Peace for all the people of the galaxy.
That was our promise. Sometimes we must take
the difficult path to achieve it. If these
rocks gave so much power to The Hushed, who
knows what this Injis could do with them."
said Lu firmly.

"Every planet had the right to opt out of the new Unity and once they exercised that right, they waived any rights to our assistance. Just as they denied us any right or jurisdiction on their worlds. I have never even heard of the planet Pharmora - it is not our business."

"This is bigger than The Unity and our self-imposed rules. Were you not listening? This war has already begun!"

"Nataalu, one of the burdens of leadership is that you cannot be all things to all people. You must choose your battles wisely. You can only do what you can do. Do not be blind to the fact that if we interfere with the affairs of other worlds, then we are becoming a dictatorship ourselves. Telling them what to do and what to think. You've let this Tam here, who incidentally we know next-to-nothing about, get inside your head. Have you not thought that he could be playing you to meet his own agenda? He said it himself. He despises the House of Royals. He is leading us into a war."

"Targole, I need not remind you that we are not the House of Royals. We are The Unity, and we will fulfil our promises. Tam has shown me what he has seen. This is a very real threat; she is coming, and we must be ready. This meeting is concluded."

"What about the vote?" asked Targole. "We are a democracy. We must vote."

"After what we have just heard here, there will be no vote. There is no choice to make.

It is our duty to protect The Unity or face certain destruction."

"My people and I had hoped to avoid conflict and move on from the violent past of our ancestors."

"And you will, we all will. Remember Targole, we fight the good fight...the alternative is the destruction of all that we have started to build here."

"Are we agreed?" asked Lu, firmly. The council stood, acknowledging their support for the action.

"Very well... how do we proceed?" asked Targole, reluctantly.

Chapter 16 — A Course of Action

"Seventeen, Zendara and Mardran," you will all go to Pharmora to investigate. We have the upper hand, the element of surprise. Do not engage her, this is a reconnaissance mission." said Tecta.

Mardran nodded her approval and added,

"May I request that Zero-Nine join us? He has proven himself a valuable member of the team on our previous missions."

"Seventeen, do you agree?," Zendara asked. Seventeen stiffened, then gave a sigh.

"If you insist Zendara, but keep him focused, he listens to you."

"Of course. I'll inform him and help prepare The Hope."

"Tecta, Pharmora doesn't even appear on any star charts post the Dawn Wars. How are we to even know where to look?" Seventeen asked quizzically.

"Gliis, you have a connection with these rocks. Have you ever tried talking back to them, or asking questions?" asked Lu.

"I wouldn't know how, they just ask me to listen. They tell me things and show me images. It is like a one-way communication."

"May I suggest The Link?" said Vrin. "The Link knows you Gliis, and their insight has served you well once before. They may also know the whereabouts of Pharmora."

"It's up to you brother, I wouldn't ask if it wasn't important," said Lu gently.

"It's okay. I trust The Link and Vrin," smiled Gliis.

"Pilot make ready Loway." He smiled, eager for more adventure.

"I will prepare my people," said Targole reluctantly. "I cannot guarantee that they will all follow."

"Targole," said Lu, placing her hand on his shoulder, "Thank you for even trying my friend. For peace."

"For peace," he replied, with the slightest of smiles.

Chapter 17 - The Link

The familiar smell of the cave's moist air and the sight of the gracefully, drifting, fungal spores and the mesmerising, pulsating walls, was a welcoming sensory overload. The environment seemed so much more inviting than the first time they had visited the Broken Crown. There was none of the apprehension or fear of the unknown. Except Pilot, he was still very wary of the walls that had beckoned him, but he did have to fight the almost irresistible urge to roll in the fungal spores again.

Gliis walked to the exact spot where he had made his first contact with The Link. He smiled as he remembered how The Link had reunited him with his mother Etala Maas. He was roused from the memory of that precious moment by Vrin's soft tones.

    "Gliis, it is time, place your hand on The Link and tell me what you see." Gliis smiled and did as Vrin asked. His eyes closed, and his breathing slowed. This was so much more

controlled than his last experience. He began
to speak, describing everything in as much
detail as he could.

"I am free falling through space in slow
motion. I see a planet shrouded in thick white
cloud, not an inch of the surface is visible.
I do not recognise this world at all."

"Don't try to work it all out Gliis, just
describe what you see and feel." Vrin's tone
was soothing.

"I am passing through the planet's
atmosphere, but I am safe. I am drifting now,
down past scores of floating buildings. They
are leisure quarters, I can see inside them.
Each of them houses zombified tourists, living
out their wildest fantasies in vivid dreams,
induced by a telepathic slumber.

Further down I go, through the false peace and
serenity of the vast deck of brilliant white
cloud. The sea of dew-coated cotton caresses
my falling body... down to the horror and
devastation of the spent, volcanic wasteland
that this planet has become - a scarred,
jagged landscape, as far as my eyes can see.
The dry matt-black of the terrain is littered
with gargantuan heaps of White Rock. I see a
workforce of slaves, people of all manner of
species, they are shifting the piles of White
Rock into openings in the ground, returning it
to where it came from. They suffer under the
watchful gaze and whiplashes of Gantuan slave
masters. I'm drifting down further still,
weaving through the mine shafts that are

carved deep into the surface. Their gaping
mouths scream in pain, the inner planet is
crying out for help.
Down deeper still... to the luminescent,
aquamarine calm of a subterranean ocean. I'm
under the water - the liquid has become
still... transformed. I am being swallowed by
the solidifying water. I'm too scared to
breathe in the translucent, gelatinous
substance that the ocean has become. It is
holding my body. I feel still, cushioned and
buoyant. Soft hands caress my cheeks and wide,
innocent eyes, hold my gaze. They are singing
out -

   "Do not panic, just breathe, you are among
friends here. We need your help Gliis. Come to
us, bring your White Rock home."

   "There is a whole species living down here,
trapped, unable to breach the surface.
Somehow, they remain tranquil, calm, patient
entities. I'm looking far into one of the
being's deep shining eyes, eyes that belie her
youthful appearance. Her gaze drops from my
eye line to look down, inviting me to do the
same. Far below us are thousands upon
thousands of the beings that populate this
aquagel. I can make out the glow of a distant
flame, it is cyan in colour but there is no
flickering. The flame is perfectly still, as
if carved from luminous rock. She is speaking
again.
   "I am my people's keeper, and we are the
guardians of the Flame of Mora. You Gliis can

set us free, and we can help save you from Injis."

"How do I help you? What should I do?" I am not speaking, this is thought projection direct to her mind. I can ask questions, I have so many questions.

"Bring the White Rock to us. Your White Rock. When you enter this cave, listen... and the rock will tell you what must be done."

"I will, I promise. Can I ask you what you know of Injis?"

"Her flame was corrupted by the black smoke of The Hushed, many thousands of years ago. The Elders of Mora told us they would contain her and never return here until they had found a cure, and more importantly, a prevention; so such a travesty could never occur again. To this day our ancestors remain in the outer reaches of space. They have failed to contain her and are unaware that she has returned. She believes if she brings enough of the White Rock home, she can create a new race of Mora in her own image. This must never come to be, and it is the reason we are still here, waiting. Together Gliis, we can defeat her and protect the flame from her corruption."
Her disc-like eyes smile at me, she is taking her gentle hands away from my face. The thick blue gel is tightening its hold on my body, I'm being forced upwards. I have breached the surface. Suddenly I'm standing on the shore, looking at an expansive beach, White Rock as far as I can see. Her words are playing over

and over in my head, "You, Gliis, can set us free."

"Well done Gliis, it's time to come back to the here and now." Vrin's soothing tones cut through the haze of his vision.

"Wait!" Gliis replied. "There is something else. IT'S TAM! Lu must get Tam to Veela VI - he doesn't have much time!"

"I feel fine" said Tam, a little panicked. Gliis broke his connection to The Link. He was in control of the exchanges with 'Them' now, a vast contrast to their last encounter.

"Tam, if you are to succeed, you must go now. Lu and Treelo must journey with you to the Mon'lal mountains."

"Are you sure I need to go?" said Lu in surprise.

"Yes Lu, I am certain."

"Taire, The Mora are still out there in space, they may be able to help us. You need to send a subspace message...."

"I'm already on it, G" said Taire, and he retreated to the pod to access the comm systems.

"Lu, please be careful."

"Aren't I always little brother? More importantly, you keep safe. Do not attempt to go to Pharmora until I return. Wait for me on Unity, we need to plan how we proceed very carefully. You are the future of The Unity little brother. I'm ~~just~~ keeping this seat warm for you."

"I will keep him close until you return

Lu," Tecta reassured her. Gliis listened to Tecta, and would never do anything to cause him trouble.

"Gliis, I know that we have already asked much of you today. I must ask you one more question though. Did the rocks tell you where Pharmora is? Seventeen was right, we cannot locate the planet on our star charts."

"No, sorry Tecta. I do not know."

"I believe that I do," said Vrin. "I know not how or why, but I know it's whereabouts. The planet we seek lies on the far side of the Zeta Belt, on the fringes of Wild Space."

"There is only one planet that far out in our galaxy and that's Exhilar, many have sought it out, very few have found it, and those that have found it, even fewer have ever returned. Most believe it's a myth," said Treelo, who looked puzzled that no one else had heard of Exhilar.

"Maybe they are one and the same," said Vrin.

Pilot had not heard a single word that had passed between his friends. The Link was tempting him, luring him in again. The pulsating lights called to him, showing him, they had a secret to tell. Something he needed to be told.

"Pilot!" Tecta's voice snapped him out of his hypnotic wandering.

"We need you to transport us back to Unity and then to take Lu and Tam on to Veela VI, the Loway is the fastest route."

"Okay, Pilot okay, yes." Pilot was dazed, but tried his best to act 'normal'.

Chapter 18 - The Genesis Sphere

Tam finally had the opportunity to fulfil his mission. He, Lu and Treelo had dropped the rest of their party on Unity and continued their journey on the Core Loway to Veela VI. Pilot was beginning to feel a bit more like his usual self, the distraction of the busy travel schedule had helped clear some of the fogginess from his mind. Bemused was the best way to describe his reaction when he learned that Tam carried the Genesis Sphere. He had spent a long moment in a deeply quizzical stare, and when he did break his silence, all he could say was:

"Friend Tam, you Father Mother both?"

"See, I'm not the only one who finds this weird," Treelo laughed, and gestured for a high five from Pilot, who left him hanging, and walked away still looking confused. Pilot hadn't forgiven Treelo for insulting Gliis at the council meeting when they first met. A fact that was abundantly clear as he refused to call him 'Friend Treelo'. He was just

Treelo, and that was the most potent insult a Pilot could offer. Pilots were small, but their ability to hold a grudge was huge. The pod tunnelled up through the rock and crumbling earth of the Veel'aan Village Square, the very spot where Pilot had met Lu, Taire and Gliis for the first time. The ground had barely settled, making the journey pretty easy going.

Tam stepped from the pod first, squinting into the sun. The familiar scent of the Veel'aan air filled his nostrils and the Sphere began to pulse in his belly; it knew they were home. Once his eyes had adjusted to the light, the scene which unveiled before his eyes moved him to tears. The Village Square was in a state of complete ruin; flashes of childhood memories came to him, and allowed him glimpses of the square in its former glory, and the vibrant souls that populated the once glorious space. This was a sight that Lu had sadly never witnessed in her time here, but her own thoughts triggered from being back here carried her back to an equally satisfying, more peaceful, innocent time.

Pilot touched Tam's hand as a sign of support. He had packed some supplies for their journey.
    "This one for Friend Lu and Friend Tam, this one you," he said, squinting at Treelo. Treelo's supply bag looked pretty sad and empty compared to the others.
    "You carry Friend Tam and Friend Lu's,"

said Pilot, insisting Treelo carry the heavier bags, and reminded him at least three times that even though he carried it, it was for Friend Tam and Friend Lu. "You carry, no for you."

"Okay I get it. No for me. I just get to be the Pack Shaa, they get the goodies. Why would I possibly mind that?" They headed off.

"Friends careful," said Pilot. "You, Pilot watch you." He shook his binox at Treelo.

Tam, Lu and Treelo were a good hour into their journey. The arid Veel'aan landscape and unrelenting sun were punishing. They painted a desolate image in the vast emptiness. Low-lying trails of dust kicked up in their wake, as their laboured steps carried them on their pilgrimage to the Mon'lal mountain range.

"I get the impression your little friend doesn't like me." said Treelo.

"To be fair, I felt that way about you when we first met too." said Tam

"Gee thanks buddy, I'm so glad I'm out here in the middle of nowhere supporting you."

"I said when we *first* met, obviously a lot has changed since then." laughed Tam.

"His name is Pilot. He's just very protective of us. We've been through a lot together." snapped Lu.

"He seems to like 'Friend Tam' just fine. I'm not a bad guy; I just have a habit of doing bad things, but only to bad people."

"You really need to work on that," said Lu

"On what?" Treelo replied, a little

offended.

"The way you portray yourself. Then maybe you'd be Friend Treelo," advised Lu.

"Not that I care what anyone thinks of me. Especially a pint-sized Pilot."

"Oh clearly," laughed Lu.

Tam had zoned out, lost in his thoughts, thoughts of Neela. She should still be here to share these moments. The trio entered the patches of scrub near the tree line at the foot of Mon'lal in silence. Something caught Lu's eye. There, glistening in the sun amidst a mess of skeletal remains, shrapnel, and leathery scraps of shrivelled Slaavene skin, was Tecta's arm. This had been the battleground for his last stand. Lu retrieved the arm, and put it into Treelo's pitiful supply bag that she carried. The other two eyed her questioningly.

"Tecta might want it," she shrugged.

* * * * * * * * * * * * * * * * *

Pilot had watched the trio trek across the dusty landscape until they were out of range of his binox. It was then that boredom and curiosity got the best of him. He couldn't shake the feeling that The Link needed to show him something. He was obsessing over it. *Pilot go back and see,* he thought. *Not take Pilot long on Loway.*

"No, Pilot no touch. Pilot no touch," he said aloud, desperately trying to convince

himself, repeating the words again and again
as he paced back and forth, kicking up the
dry, dusty ground.

"Pilot no touch, Pilot no touch, Pilot no
touch." His co-pilot, Pilot, stuck his head
out of the boarding hatch.

"Pilot no touch what?"

"Pilot no touch, Pilot no touch." He was
stuck in a frenzied loop.

"PILOT NO TOUCH WHAT!" this time he
shouted.

"PILOT STOP, PILOT MAKE DUST STORM" He
laughed nervously, trying to make light of the
situation, but Pilot wasn't hearing him at
all. He walked up to Pilot and slapped him
across the back of the head. Pilot stopped in
his tracks, stunned, and then slapped him
back. The slap-off that followed escalated
into a full-on scuffle, which resulted in them
both rolling around on the dusty ground.

"NO MORE!" shouted a croaky-voiced third
Pilot, who had emerged from the pod.

"Why you hit Pilot?"

"Him head problems," said Pilot the co-
pilot.

"He no hear, I slap, he hear."

"Why head problems you?," asked the
croaky-voiced Pilot.

"Pilot must go Link," said Pilot.

"Why?"

"Link need Pilot to see."

"What see?"

"Pilot not know."

"Ah that why you say, 'Pilot no touch.'

Pilot scared of Link?" said co-pilot.

"Pilot not scared." He puffed his chest out defiantly.

"Pilots go Link now."

"But friend Lu," said the croaky Pilot.

"Pilots come back, Loway fast, friend Lu be here still."

"Come, come, Pilots go now."

* * * * * * * * * * * * * * * * * * * *

The route through Mon'lal was tough-going, but the Sphere kept them on track. It was like Tam had a built-in compass, which was their guide through the caves and crevices of the mountain range. It seemed like they had been negotiating the slick-walled caves for hours, when Tam finally stopped. He pointed to an opening in the rock from which light spilled into the dank, cavernous darkness that surrounded them. One at a time, they squeezed through the narrow opening and found themselves in a clearing, enclosed on all sides by sheer rock faces. The dense rock extended upwards to dizzying heights, hundreds of feet above their standpoint. The Cradle was suspended high above them, and beyond that, at the crest of the rock faces, there was piercing blue, cloudless sky.

"So how do we get up there?" Treelo wore a puzzled expression as he looked up at the Cradle.

"We really don't need to," said Lu. Tam

was levitating. The Genesis Sphere was being drawn up to the Cradle, carrying Tam with it.

"Don't panic Tam, trust the Sphere," Lu reassured him.

"I'm okay, just a little nervous about how the Sphere is going to be removed."

That comment from Tam would usually be Treelo's cue to make an ill-advised joke, but he was too nervous to do so.

The light from the Sphere pulsed beneath Tam's tunic. His arms and legs were drawn out to the sides and secured by the Cradle. It locked him in a star jump position, hands and feet connected to the rock faces. The Sphere's light burned bright in Tam's belly, then it travelled the length of his arms and legs, pulsing and rushing out of his body into the rock. All of ~~the~~ a sudden, the glow of the Genesis Sphere became erratic, the flow of power appeared broken, disrupted somehow.

"Something's wrong!" Tam shouted, his head dropped, and his body slumped in the Cradle. The Genesis Sphere grew dim.

"Tam!" Lu shouted, "Can you hear me?" Tam was unresponsive. Lu had equipped her combat suit before the mission, but she hadn't anticipated she would be using it in this way. The flexible, armoured, second skin was even more versatile than the previous model. Taire had spared no imagination in the upgrade. Lu ran and jumped at the vertical rock face. As her foot contacted the harsh surface - she pushed off vertically, and the suit switched from Regular to Low G mode, which catapulted her towards Tam. She threw her arms around his neck and steadied herself. Pressed close to him, she set her gravity emitters to hover.

"I've got you," she whispered in his ear, and pressed her forehead against his. Tam gasped, the sharp intake of air jolted him awake. Lu's energy was acting like a backup power cell. Tam's exhausted body was enlivened, they lit up in unison as the Sphere's energy transfer resumed. The last remnants of the Sphere's power left Tam's body, and the Cradle released him. Lu lowered him gently down to the ground. Treelo had watched the spectacle helplessly, he realised he had hardly taken a breath for its duration. He was poised, ready to catch Tam and Lu as they descended, assuming they would be spent from the exertion of the ordeal. He was pleasantly surprised to watch their controlled touchdown and to see them both standing firm, smiling at each other, then at him.

"Wow!! That was.... something. Are you both okay?"

"Great, the best I've felt in a long time. I thought I would feel empty, but instead I am filled with another feeling that I can't quite give a name to yet." Lu blushed at Tam's words. They both felt energised, replenished and contented. Specks of warm rain began to fall. They looked skyward, and the clear blue patch of sky that had been above them earlier had turned midnight black. Thunder roared, and lightning cracked, which illuminated the heavens. The rock faces that surrounded the Cradle lit up with the luminous green energy of the Sphere; it streaked within the rock face like contained fork lightning. The spits of rain quickly developed into a torrent, that hammered down not just on Mon'lal, but across the entirety of Veela VI. The neon-green light spread from the walls of the Cradle, and sprawled across the surface of the planet like a network of veins and arteries carrying life-giving blood through a living body. A new beginning had been set in motion, the next chapter in the life of this once derelict planet had begun. The scent of summer rain on parched earth filled the air. They were witnessing a miracle. The three of them sheltered in the entrance of the cave system, and enjoyed the wonder of what they had set in motion. A flicker turned into a glow, and there before them were holographic images of Tamara and Ambrion, Tam's parents. Tamara began to speak.

"Tam, our beloved son. If you are seeing this message, then you have succeeded in your mission. We are so very proud of you. You have set a miracle in motion. The Genesis Sphere is breathing new life into Veela VI, restoring the planet to its original beauty. This event will trigger the activation of scores of bio-pods that have been planted across the planet. Now they will gestate and bare young adult Veel'aans, pre-taught and conditioned with one objective: to restart our species. The Sphere will also act as a beacon, calling any surviving Veel'aans home."

"We feel pride beyond any words that you have fulfilled your mission, our son. You are the saviour of the Veel'aan way of life and we love you so very much, may the future treat you well." As soon as Ambrion had said his piece, the hologram ended abruptly.

Tears stood in Tam's reddened eyes. He finally understood... he was proud of his parent's sacrifice and of himself.

"So, now can I call you hero?" Treelo laughed, but this time it was meant as a compliment. He was actually proud of what Tam had achieved, and his own small part in helping him fulfil his mission.

Despite the miracle that Tam had just performed, they were all keenly aware that their next mission had barely begun. They were going to have to fight to protect this place, as well as the rest of The Unity. Now Tam had something tangible to fight for, he was more determined than ever that he would not take the passive stance that his people took in the Twenty Four-Hour War. It was the correct route for his people at that time, and they had succeeded in this most recent trial, but the war was coming, and they needed to get back to Unity to prepare.

As they walked, the trio collectively had the sense that they were treading on virgin ground. Veela VI was almost unrecognisable, only the largest landmarks were familiar. They began the trek through the vibrant new-born foliage and lush vegetation, that was still in the process of growing around them. By the time the Village Square was in sight, night had fallen. The Veel'aan sunset had been unlike any other that Tam or Lu had ever witnessed, it was spectacular, bordering on the psychedelic. As the deep red sun melted into the horizon, it gave way to the twin moons rising through an orange and purple haze of the departing storm clouds. The moons hung majestically in the evening sky, peering mistily through the shroud of wispy cloud cover that remained. How Lu had missed them. She was filled with the warmth of knowing she was home, for at least a short while.

"Tam, I've been meaning to ask you, what happened to Veela One through to Five?" questioned Treelo.

"Good question. You'd have thought they were discovered first. However, that my friend is incorrect. It simply comes down to the fact that our planet was discovered in the sixth month of the calendar year, by a team of six Astro Voyagers."

"Bit weird," answered Treelo. "Much like everything else I've seen on this planet."

"Treelo," said Lu, "In a lot of ways, I'm equally as alien to this planet as you. Although it is my biological people's home planet and the place where I grew up, I always assumed I was a surrogate citizen. It was only later, and thanks to Vrin, that I found out I

was actually born of this world, and the more
I have learned, the more curious and
fascinating I have found this place."

They reached the almost unrecognizable Village
Square. It was packed full of lush foliage and
the ancient statues had been adorned with
flowering climbing plants. This addition gave
them a new kind of beauty.

"So, this is the rendezvous point, but
where's Pilot?" said Lu.

"Well that's the maze, he dropped us just
there to the left...but there's no trace of
the breach point," said Treelo, who looked
puzzled.

"The planet has been reborn. Scars have
been healed," said Tam.

"But still, where is Pilot? He wouldn't
leave us behind," spoke Lu, with a hint of
concern in her voice.

"Well if he did leave, it must be for a
very good reason. He pretty much worships you
two."

"Treelo, you almost sound jealous,"
laughed Tam.

"I'm not jealous, I just don't understand
why he hates me so much."

"Let's be rational here, Pilot would only
leave us if it was essential, and he would
never abandon us. He will be back," said Lu.
"We need to make camp, it will soon be too
dark to see properly. We should light a fire
at least and make ourselves comfortable whilst
we wait. Anyone else hungry?"

"Yes, I'm starving. Some of us got more supplies than others, namely you two."

"I was eating for two," laughed Tam.

"Some of these vines must bear fruit. I'll go forage, care to join me Tam?" asked Lu

"Yeah, sure. I'm useless at lighting fires. Treelo is the practical one."

"That's fine by me, I love a good fire." Treelo busied himself, gathering kindling and tinder.

As Lu and Tam wandered through the lush vegetation, they gathered various fruits and berries. Lu had an ulterior motive when she had asked Tam to join her. She craved the connection they had shared and wanted more; she hoped he felt the same way.
Tam was irked by his feelings of guilt about Neela, but he couldn't deny his passion and desire for Lu. She made him feel complete. The two of them skirted around their unspoken feelings with small talk, as they plucked ripe fruit from the abundance of vines.

"Look at the moons, I've missed this view," said Tam awkwardly.

"I'd rather look at you and see you look back at me, the way you did that first night on Unity." Lu couldn't hold back any longer. The two of them stood face-to-face beneath the twin moons, the fragrance of the floral blooms enhanced the fertile ambience. They embraced, the light ignited within their beings once more. Nataalu caressed Tam's cheek with her flawless fingers and pressed her lips to his. Tam returned the kiss, the sweet warmth of their tongues intertwined, and their heightened senses tingled; once again they felt whole. The earth literally moved beneath their feet in a burst of vibration.

"Guys, did you feel that?" Treelo shouted. "Erm...you really need to come back and see this." Treelo was sat by his fire, looking beyond the maze. He had spotted movement, something new had appeared, some kind of structure. It was a low, circular wall, about twenty feet in diameter and of seemingly simple design. It appeared to be a part of the planet surface, as if carved from one giant piece of rock. Lu and Tam broke off their embrace and ran toward Treelo, using the distant glow of his fire as a homing beacon. Treelo was on his feet, waiting when they arrived at the clearing in the square.
    "Did you feel the tremor?" asked Treelo. "It happened when *that* appeared." The three of them passed slowly through the square to cautiously approach the wall. As they did so, it grew taller. This wasn't a trick of perception; the wall was actually getting higher. Treelo took a couple of uncertain backward steps. As he did so, the wall lowered again.
    "Unless I'm hugely mistaken," said Tam, "This is…"
    "The Eye from Veel'aan legend," Lu

finished. "I believe you are right Tam."
Lu approached the wall, and reached out to
touch the surface.

Chapter 19 - Contact

The Hope approached the coordinates Vrin had provided, and there it was, the mysterious planet that had caused such confusion. It was steeped in cloud cover, so thick that it obscured the entire surface from view. The Hope's sensors chimed.

"What was that?" Zendara was referring to a short burst of energy that had caused the alarm to sound.

"Space debris, a discarded energy cell. Nothing to concern us," Seventeen reassured her.

"We have, as The Unitians say, 'Bigger oogmah to boil'" Zero- Nine chipped in, then roared with laughter at his own joke.

"For the record Zero-Nine, I have never heard any Unitia…"

Seventeen was cut off mid-sentence when the ship jolted violently. His console exploded into a mess of sparks and smoke. The impact threw Seventeen and Zendara backwards into the rear wall of the bridge. Smoke continued to belch from the flight control console, where Mardran was fighting the flight stick to keep the ship level. For once, instead of being slightly embarrassed by her 'irrational over-the-top seat belt obsession,' she felt thankful and justified in her obsessiveness. Sadly, there was no time to revel in her small personal victory. A dense blue-grey smog had filled the bridge, with the sour stench of electrical fire. None of them could see anything.

"Mardran, are you okay?" asked Seventeen.

"Yes! But I could do with some help. The stabilisers have been hit and need to be realigned," she shouted, as she struggled to make her small voice heard over the deafening alarms.

"Zendara, are you injured?" Seventeen shouted. ~~But~~ She didn't reply. "Zendara, tell me that you are okay?" demanded Seventeen. She had been knocked unconscious by her impact with the bulkhead. She lay slumped in a crumpled heap on the deck.
Zero-Nine knelt on the floor next to her, and performed some medical scans.

"Zee will be okay," he said with relief in his tone. "I am fine too Seventeen. Thank you for your concern. So glad you asked. Oh that's right, you didn't."

"We don't have time for this Zero-Nine, extinguish that fire now," he ordered.

"No, I'm looking after Zee. You extinguish the fire and help Mardran."
Seventeen had never known Zero-Nine to be so

emotional and directly insubordinate. Inappropriate and rude, yes, but insubordinate, never. It became clear that he genuinely cared for Zendara. Seventeen didn't argue, he told Mardran to take a deep breath and hit the purge button, which was usually employed to cleanse the life support systems after a mission. The absence of oxygen swiftly suffocated the fire, and in an instant, the ship was free of smoke and re-pressurised. Seventeen, who had no need for oxygen, had been recalibrating The Hope's stabilisers whilst the smoke cleared. Mardran took a deep breath of the clean air. She continued to wrestle with the flight stick.

"Well held Mardran, the controls should become a lot more manageable momentarily. The smoke cleared and Mardran shouted,

"Seventeen, look!" He looked out just in time to catch what must've been the ship which had fired upon them. It pierced Exhilar's atmosphere in a fiery burst, to get swallowed into the thick cloud below.

"What happened?" said Zendara groggily, as she tried to sit up.

"Slowly," said Zero-Nine gently, as he helped her.

"We will fill you in when we figure it out, but first you need to be checked out. Zero-Nine, help Zendara to the Med Bay. I will contact Tecta." Zendara was too dazed to argue, but Zero-Nine wasn't.

"What do you think I'm doing already?" he snapped.

"Zero," said Seventeen, "I apologise, and for the record, it pleases me that you are okay."

"About time I was appreciated," sneered Zero-Nine, as he led Zendara to the Med Bay.

"I will update Tecta on developments and plan our next move," said Seventeen.

Chapter 20 — True Pilots

The Loway pod arrived at The Link and Pilot wasted no time. He burst from the boarding hatch and rushed to the glowing wall, he thrust his stumpy hand inside. He was immersed in a vision immediately. The Link showed him Injis' army. They were instantly recognisable to him, they were Scavengers, who had destroyed his planet *Home*.

"No! Pilots, they with she."

"Who with she, Pilot?" asked the co-pilot.

"Home killers, Scavengers." The Link went on to show him something he truly wished it hadn't. The images were of a Protector Droid being devoured by The Hunger.

"Friend Protectors die." Pilot had tears pouring from his eyes. He wished he could unsee the devastating images that had been forever burned into his mind's eye. He stepped away from the wall, he had seen enough. Pilot asked the croaky-voiced Pilot to call all Pilots to meet - his tone was uncharacteristically solemn. Moments later, a sea of Pilots filled the cave. They chirped and chattered in a mix of apprehension and total confusion.

"Pilots listen, Pilot!" shouted croaky-voiced Pilot. A hush fell over the crowd.

"This Pilot Council, for vote." Pilot spoke his next words with pure defiance.

"Friend Tecta save all Pilots, now Pilots must save Friend Protectors. Pilots go, Pilots fight!" His ever-buoyant spirit had reasoned that nothing was set in stone, and he would do everything he could to save his friends.

"Pilot's no weapons," said an older Pilot, at the front of the crowd.

"Pilots brave, Pilot's brains smart weapons, trust Pilot."

"Who save friend Protectors!?" he shouted.

"Pilots!" they shouted in unison. It was a shoddily-organised vote, but nonetheless, it was a vote for action.

"Pilot, what is going on here?" A deep metallic voice boomed and echoed about the cave. Fifty-Six had been listening to the vote, if you could call it that. He had stayed with Pilots on the Core Loway after the activation of the Unity Spire. The truth was that he had felt redundant for far too long, and his fellow Protectors had wrapped him up in cotton wool. He had been tasked with mundane jobs, they had refused to put him in the face of danger. Fifty-Six had been damaged in the Dawn Wars, he wasn't useless or fragile, but that was exactly how they had made him feel. He felt that he had much less to lose than his brethren. He'd lost his mobility, yes, but he was far from helpless.

"Friend Fifty-Six, Pilots must fight. Not for revenge, for friend Protectors."

"What have you seen in this place Pilot?"

"Friend Protectors much danger, bad weapon eat metal, you metal."

"You have my word, I will help you, if you just let me fight with you. I need this more than you could ever know."

"No safe for metal, Friend Fifty-Six metal," said Pilot. "No, no, no safe you."

"Don't worry about me, we have to prepare you my friend. I have something you need to see."

"Okay, but you no tell friend Protectors, Pilot plans."

Fifty-Six led Pilots back to the pod. He was filled with an exhilaration he'd not felt in more than a decade. He had a strong bargaining

chip up his sleeve, and he was about to play
it. He would once again be where he belonged,
in the heart of battle.

Chapter 21 - Hornets

Fifty-Six led Pilot through the barren sectors of the Core Loway. They were headed to a disused launch bay. Pilots were small and didn't take up much room, and they were also very economical in their use of space, energy and resources. They had only ever used what they needed, and everything that they had ever needed was in the few sections of the Loway that they had made their home. Much of the Loway hadn't been explored for years, and there was far more to this place than anyone could imagine.

"Where we go friend, no things in here?" said Pilot.

"Friend Pilot, when you first welcomed me here to your home, we were on a mission to release the Tek." said Fifty-Six.

"Okay, Pilot know this."

"In that moment, when we activated the Tek and played our part in the victory over The Hushed, I regained a sense of purpose. I realised that I could still be a useful Protector. On that day I made a pledge to myself: that I would help you and your people to protect yourselves against any future threats. I wanted to do this to repay the kindness and generosity you have shown me. Through inviting me to live here with you, you have become my family, and the Loway has become my home. What I found in here, behind these doors, has made my promise much easier to fulfil."

Pilot looked at him a little confused. Fifty-Six opened the doors to the launch bay, and Pilot's expression transformed from puzzlement, to one of wonder and amazement. The bay was filled with Pilot-sized vehicles, solid machines, copper bronze in colour. They sported razor-sharp core drills at the nose, diamond-tipped, with titanium grinding plates. These drills could slice and grind their way through any substance, no matter how dense.

    "Pilot, these were Scout Drills; single-person vehicles with diamond shielding. They are constructed of raw gold and other solid precious metals - they are virtually indestructible."

    "Pilots not know dis treasure here."

    "They are literally treasure my friend. The materials they are built from were easily available to the Core Miners that came before you. Their component parts are worth billions of credits, but these little ships now have an invaluable purpose. I have modified them to fit Pilots perfectly. I cut out the bulky back-end and modified the boosters. These little beasts can travel underground or underwater, up in the air, or in space. Pilot, you and your fellow Pilots will now be able to protect yourselves. I call them Hornets, on account of their colour and the lethal sting of the nose-mounted drill."

Fifty-Six looked down at Pilot, who was hugging his leg and sobbing.

"Pilot, do you not like them?"

"Thank you, Friend Fifty-Six, Pilot happy, but sad."

"Why sad?"

"You protect Pilots, I not no if Pilots can save Friend."

"Pilot, you have already saved me. I have fulfilled my purpose. You could give me no greater gift. Now let's go blow up some bad people."

* * * * * * * *

The bold, angular, Black Palace imposed itself menacingly over the surface of Exhilar. The sculpted lava rock structure was Injis's base of operation. From its harsh, spiked battlements, she could oversee the process of the White Rock being returned to the cave systems. This was also the vantage point from which Injis would rule over her soon-to-be-born *Order of the White Rock*. The Black Palace was carved from an ancient volcanic lava flow, and the structure was eerily beautiful. It appealed to Injis on a number of levels. It's imposing dark form matched her essence, and the palatial grandeur and majesty appealed to her inner-child; the princess that never was. She wasn't given the chance to play and experience the care-free nature of youth. After millennia, she was still a bitter child at heart, with a chip on her shoulder and the insatiable hunger for more that children possess. *This time,* she thought, *I will have my own way.*

"Vrex, you have done well here, you will be rewarded accordingly."

"Thank you, my glorious leader."

"This is an act of devious genius; not only have you tamed the Gantuans, you have also created what is now known as Exhilar. All manner of people pay large sums of credits to visit this planet of euphoria, to breathe the atmosphere and immerse themselves in their most unsavoury fantasies. I have heard it is a most addictive high. The real brilliance however, lies down here in the dark underbelly. You have pitched it to the perfect demographic. The undesirables, miscreants and callous thrill- seekers, the ones who will do whatever it takes to make it here. The ones who will go unnoticed if they should never return. Abducting them and putting them to work here was a stroke of genius. Soon we will be ready to begin again."

From out of nowhere, the ground beneath their feet quaked and shuddered.

"Vrex, what is happening?" snapped Injis. Vrex's comm link chimed.

"Sir, we have intercepted a subspace transmission, a message to The Mora. It is a call for help, originating from The Planet Unity."

"How is this possible? If they know what we are doing here, we will need to bring our plans forward. Time is still on our side. The Mora will never receive that message in time to affect anything, they are light years from here. Still, we must attack now." Vrex stood gaping.

"Vrex, are you listening to me?"

"Mistress, it would seem that they have brought the attack to us." The Hornets burrowed up from Exhilar's core like lethal copper-coloured darts. They burst through the planet's surface to attack the Scavengers and the Black Palace.

"Get to The Vengeance now!" growled Injis. She was enraged that she had been outmanoeuvred.

Fifty-Six burst from the bore tunnel that Pilot's Hornet had carved. He set about freeing the Slaves, who instantly revolted, bludgeoning their Gantuan slave masters with rocks and their bare hands.

"No!" screamed Pilot, "Friend Fifty-Six, no safe. Stay inside." Fifty-Six ignored Pilot's pleading; he would be the Protector he knew he could be. He charged through numerous Scavengers, flailing his solid arms as he

went. The Scavengers, broken by Fifty-Six's
crushing blows, were sent flying this way and
that in a mess of blood and broken bones.
Their devastated bodies lay strewn about the
rocky ground. He freed a number of slaves who
in turn went about freeing their fellow
captives.

"Get to the tunnels, you are free," Fifty-
Six shouted his instructions to the liberated
slaves. He told them to keep travelling
downward and not to return, no matter how long
it took for him to rejoin them.

"You will be saved this day." He bellowed
the words with a pride he hadn't felt since
the first battle of Unity, so many years
before. A Gantuan whip wrapped around his
wrist. He trapped it in his hand and gave a
short powerful tug. The Gantuan at the other
end of the whip flew through the air on a
collision course with Fifty-Six, to be met
with the full force of his solid metal fist -
slamming into his face. The Gantuan was
reduced to a mess of snot, gore and shattered
bone.

"This is what I was made for!" shouted
Fifty-Six, his voice was filled with joy. Two
more Gantuans charged at him, whips hissing
and cracking ferociously in the air. Fifty-Six
clenched his fists which activated his wrist
sabres. The vicious blades gleamed in the
sunlight, in a flash he had sliced through the
pair of whips that threatened to ensnare him.
He retracted the twin sabres, it had been a
long time since he had engaged in hand to hand

combat, *I'm going to enjoy this*. The Gantuan's
rushed him simultaneously. He stepped across
himself with his right leg and delivered a
heavy blow to the ribs of the first Gantuan.
Fifty-Six used his momentum to spin full
circle, he unleashed a brutal back fist strike
to the side of the second Gantuan's head.
*These things skulls are thicker than Lardorien
Fog.* The first Gantuan had regained his
breath, he attacked Fifty-Six with the stub
that remained of his electro whip. It
contained enough charge to deliver a shock
strong enough, that it momentarily jolted the
droid. Fifty-Six shook of the charge and
roared. He pummelled his attacker with a
relentless barrage of punches, reducing him to
a scarlet splurge on the rocks. The second
Gantuan had taken advantage of Fifty-Six's
preoccupation with battering his fellow
warrior. He stomped on the back of Fifty-Six's
good leg, which forced him down on one knee.
The Gantuan set about bashing in Fifty-Six's
head with a pair of blunt rocks. The droid's
casing was too robust to be compromised by the
primal attack. He reached back behind his head
and grabbed the Gantuan by both wrists, he
twisted his body so he faced his foe, placed
his good foot in the Gantuan's mid-riff and
pushed away while keeping both hands tightly
gripped on the reptilian's wrists. With a rip,
crack and a sickening crunch, the Gantuan's
body, devoid of it's arms was sent flying
backwards into an unrelenting rocky outcrop.
His body was shattered. The slaves, spurred on

by Fifty-Six's relentless onslaught, rushed the Scavenger army. Fifty-Six stood, full of pride and set about beating the Scavenger's with the heavy severed arms of the defeated Gantuan.

Fifty-Six could see Injis beyond the crowd. He had his sights set firmly on her: she knew she stood no chance going toe-to-toe with a Protector Droid. She could clearly see that he was winning, and he would come for her next.

"End him!" she screamed at her Scavenger guards. She managed to retain an air of composure as she retreated and boarded The Vengeance. Vrex spat covering fire as its engines boomed, lifting it off from the parched black surface.

"Unleash The Hunger on my current coordinates," ordered Injis. The Vengeance tilted to direct its nose toward the sky; with a whine and a deafening roar, it shot upward like an archer's arrow fired from a taught bow.

High above the planet, a lone missile broke Wild Space and screamed through Exhilar's atmosphere. It moved so quickly that Seventeen and his crew had no time to react. The missile sped towards the Black Palace and Fifty-Six, (who was surrounded by the broken bodies of the Scavenger guards and Gantuan's that he and the freed slaves had defeated.) Pilot had clocked the missile. He aimed his ship towards it and engaged full thrust, the diamond-tipped cone drill on the front of his Hornet squealed as it spun to full momentum. He closed in on the missile. There was an unexpected thud and a shudder; Pilot had been so absorbed with taking out the missile, that he had failed to see an inbound mortar bolt... it had scored a direct hit on the flank of his ship. The physical damage it caused was negligible, but the impact had been enough to knock his Hornet off-course. He wrestled with the controls, desperate to correct his path to the missile. It wasn't enough, his fighter only managed to graze the weapon's tail fin, which caused it to deviate only slightly from its course. His heart sank. The Link had already shown him what would happen next... Pilot watched helplessly as the missile detonated metres from Fifty-Six. The Hunger was upon him instantly. The dense, ancient, alloy of his body gave way under the ferocity of the attack. Pilot exited his Hornet, and ran to his friend as fast as his short legs would carry him. Numerous other Pilots followed his lead, and joined him in trying to scrape the insidious weapon from Fifty-Six's body. It was hopeless... he was being eaten alive.

   "Pilot so sorry friend." His thick tears streamed uncontrollably as he continued to scrape at The Hunger, which now invaded Fifty-Six's face.

   "Don't be sorry my friend. What good is a Protector who isn't allowed to protect? You gave me purpose. Thank you for making me feel alive again."

"Pilots no forget you." Fifty-Six was gone, totally consumed. All that remained was the residue of The Hunger, and even that dissolved swiftly into nothing.

Pilot made a heart-wrenching howl, filled with loss and despair. His howls were met by those of every other Pilot around him.

"This enough!" shouted Pilot.

"Pilots lose no more Friends." said co-pilot.

"Pilots go space, Pilots fight," said the croaky Pilot.

"No for revenge no! For friends and peace!" shouted Pilot. A rapturous roar filled the air. Pilots ran to their Hornets and powered them up, ready for battle. They tore into the sky like missiles launched from a silo, punching holes in the cloud deck as they screamed spaceward.

Chapter 22 - From The Edge

"Slaavene fleet to Unity fleet, do not fire upon us, we repeat, do not fire upon us. We stand with you."

"Slither with whoever is winning more like," Mardran commented off comms.

"We copy you, Slaavene fleet," Seventeen replied. "Glad to have you onside."

"The enemy believes that we are with them. They are in for a surprise," hissed the Slaavene pilot.

"Typical slippery Slaavene" said Mardran, clucking her tongue.

"We need all the help we can get Mardran, however questionable."

"That's true enough, but don't ask me to trust them."

"Copy that Slaavene fleet. We have been fired upon by a single ship, although we sustained only superficial damage. Our support fleet from Unity is imminent. It is good to have you onside," Seventeen continued his exchange.

"...and I thought you Protectors couldn't lie," smiled Mardran.

"I believe the term is needs must, my friend. Besides, there is more going on here than meets the eye. We are a single ship, and a long way from home. If the Slaavene had wanted to destroy us, they would've seized the opportunity."

"You're the boss, but for the record, I don't like it one bit." The Slaavene vessels formed up alongside The Hope. The new alliance watched and waited in edgy silence.

"There, eleven o'clock." Mardran had spotted The Vengeance break the cloud deck.

"On my command," said Seventeen evenly. "Hold."
The Vengeance tore away from Exhilar and headed toward the edge of the galaxy. "Hold!" repeated Seventeen. To his surprise, Injis' ship performed a sweeping corkscrew manoeuvre, and came to a halt just shy of the threshold to Wild Space. The Vengeance had turned about face, and now hung menacingly in the distance. The vivid swirling colours of Wild Space created a beautiful backdrop for the angular black and chrome ship.

"She's waiting... but for what?" The question wasn't rhetorical. Tecta was open to suggestions.

"Unity ship, they are toying with us. We must attack," the Slaavene Commander snapped at Seventeen, impatiently.

"Hold," Seventeen repeated. "Something about this does not feel right." However, the Slaavene fighters made their move. Zero-Nine entered the bridge with a slightly bruised, but otherwise okay, Zendara.

"Seventeen, I think your instincts have served us well," he spoke in a deadly serious tone. Even he couldn't make a joke of what his scans were showing. A mammoth fleet of ships were about to breach the edge of space... on a collision course with the onrushing Slaavene fleet.

"Slaavene fleet, ABORT OFFENSIVE STRIKE! ABORT!"

"It is one small ship, we cannot fail," came the reply. The Slaavene were deep into their attack run when Injis's fleet breached the threshold of Unity space. An awe-inspiring wall of Destroyers and Battlecruisers formed up behind The Vengeance, then stopped. The Slaavene fleet screamed to a halt. The scene that followed resembled a space age version of a wild west standoff. A barbed tension and heavy silence filled the void between them. Both sides anxiously waited for the other to show the slightest twitch, or giveaway, that they were about to open fire.

The standoff was broken by the swarm of Hornets. They sliced through the clouds and burst into space, directly between the Slaavene and Injis's fleet.

"Friends no shoot, Pilots help," came the familiar voice through all friendly comm channels.

"Pilot, how are you even out here? ~~and~~
Where did you get those ships?" Seventeen was
genuinely stunned by the spectacle.

"Scout Drills. Friend Fifty-Six help make
gooder for space. Friend Fifty-Six gone, you
need go, no safe."

"The Core Loway really is the gift that
keeps on giving," Zero chipped in.

"Pilots no called Pilots for nothing. You
need go now. Weapon eat metal. Tell Tecta."
Pilot was getting frustrated. Seventeen and
his crew weren't understanding what Pilot was
trying to tell them.

The Slaavene fleet powered up and followed
Pilot's Hornets at full attack speed. A volley
of missiles tore from Injis's Destroyers: The
Hunger was imminent again. The Slaavene ships
spat laser cannon bolts and scores of missiles
in the general direction of Injis and her
fleet. The fleet was unnervingly static,
unmoved by the wall of fire that approached
them. The Hornets dodged and weaved their way
through the friendly fire of the Slaavene
ships, as they hunted down The Hunger's
carrying missiles.
One of the Hornets locked onto an enemy
missile and sliced clean through it, as if it
wasn't even there. The Hunger spilled out of
the breached missile onto the Hornet. The vile
substance couldn't get any purchase on its
diamond-shielded surface, like oil trying to
cling to a non-stick pan, the lethal liquid

slid helplessly away but straight into the path of an incoming Slaavene fighter. The Hunger was upon the fighter in an instant, gorging itself on its high gloss metal surface. In minutes it had reduced the ship to nothing. The Slaavene pilot and gunner flailed their serpentine limbs in panic, but within seconds, they had succumbed to the sub-zero vacuum of space.

"What kind of weapon is that?" asked Mardran, totally freaked out by the horror of the spectacle.

"I do not know, but it's eating through those Slaavene fighters like sugar floss," said Zendara, who had regained some of her usual composure.

"Pilot, get out of there!" commanded Seventeen.

"Pilots okay, Pilot ship no metal shields. Pilots fight, weapon eat metal, eat friend Fifty-Six. You need go, now!!"

"What is he talking about?" asked Zero.

"Zero, what material are Seventeen, yourself, and this ship constructed from?" snapped Zendara.

"Metal!" shouted Zero.

"Fall back," ordered Seventeen. "Slaavene fleet, fall back now." It was too late - their comms were dead. The entire Slaavene fleet had been consumed. All that remained were the floating popsicle corpses of the crews.

"Mardran, get us out of here, there's nothing we can do to help them. Staying here would be suicide, and the Pilots have given us a chance to escape," ordered Seventeen.

"A chance? I believe the term is that they are kicking arse," said Zero.

Pilots had flown headlong into Injis's fleet, using the weapons fire which was the final act of the Slaavene as a distraction. The Hornets were too small to be picked off by the Destroyers, they were wreaking havoc, carving gaping holes in the enemy ships, breaching hulls and decks.

"What are these vermin?" screamed Injis. "Destroy them."

"We can't lock onto their shields," seethed Vrex, "And they are too small to target manually." The Hornets continued their assault. They took out proto-cannons, weapons arrays and completely destroyed some of the smaller ships of the fleet. The awesome little Hornets did have one weakness; a short power supply. They were running perilously low, and needed to return to the Loway to replenish their charge.

"Pilots, good fight. We go Loway now. Charge Hornets," said Pilot breathlessly.

"Friend Seventeen safe?" asked the co-pilot.

"Safer now, they have chance. Pilot must go Veela VI. Friend Lu need us help." They made one final pass in chaotic formation, and tore through the thrusters of The Vengeance as they went. Injis, who was jolted by the impact, was enraged. Her cyan flames fired like solar flares.

"All of this firepower and you're telling me we have no defence against this miniscule annoyance," she shrieked.

"We've tried everything, even ramming them, but they are too fast and manoeuvrable. The Hunger cannot penetrate their shields. We might as well be spitting at them." Vrex winced as he waited for her response. Instead of the rage-filled barrage of criticism that he had anticipated, a hush fell. The only exceptions were the sporadic crackles and booms as the explosions petered out.

"Mistress Injis, they have retreated."

"Assess the damage, I need to be mobile. I feel a change of tactics is called for; now they know that I am here, and what numbers I have. We will take the fight to the heart of what they love most, the planet Unity...and Vrex..."

"Yes Mistress."

"Find a way to stop those irritating bugs, in case they are foolish enough to return for a second bite at my fleet."

"Hound One, are you receiving me?" Vrex hailed the Scavenger ship.

"Yes Vengeance, what were those things?" Vrex ignored the question.

"Did The Hunger destroy the Protector ship?" he asked, hopefully.

"Negative, but we did get their heading and our systems are tracking them."

"That is disappointing, but at least it's

something. All tactical leads convene and study those micro fighters, by the time we next engage the enemy, I want a concrete solution to stop them." Vrex switched to open comms. "Attention fleet, all hands to repair stations, make haste. We have a hunt to get underway. Hound, keep tracking them, and as soon as you are mobile, follow their heading. Stay close, but not too close."

Chapter 23 – A Dark Command

"Seventeen to Unity, are you receiving me? Over. You must evacuate the planet immediately."

"Seventeen, this is Taire, what's going on?"

"Get everyone to the Broken Crown. Injis and a massive fleet are pursuing us. The Slaavene fleet is gone."

"What were the Slaavene doing there? And what do you mean gone?"

"No time to explain. Pilots showed up in fighters and bought us some time to get away."

"What?"

"I know! Contact Pilot. His ships were the only thing that survived Injis's weapon. It literally eats metal."

"And guess who's made of metal?" Zero shouted in the background.

"Eats metal?!! What? And Pilot was supposed to be on Vee'la VI with Lu!"

"Taire! Contact Pilot now! His ships may be the key to our survival." snapped Seventeen.

* * * * * * * * * * * * *

"Tecta to Seventeen, the evacuation to the Broken Crown is underway. I also have a plan, although I know you are not going to like it."

"A plan is good! We're taking suggestions."

"Quiet Zero. Go ahead Tecta."

"Sorry if I'm understandably nervous," mumbled Zero.

"Lead Injis and her fleet to Feer'aal. The Feruccians will not tolerate any trespass in their space. Use their inevitable counter attack as a distraction to get away, and meet us at the Broken Crown."

"But we'd be condemning the whole planet to death. We are Protectors, not killers!" Seventeen was mortified.

"We are Protectors of The Unity, not Feer'aal, and as a Protector, you will follow orders. Sometimes, however hard it may be, we need to take a step back to enable us to move forwards, for peace. May the Mother forgive us for our actions on this day."

"Tecta, I will not force Mardran to attack her own peo…"
Mardran cut him off.

"As a R'aal, I no longer consider Feer'aal my home, or the Feruccians to be my people. They love war, thrive on it, so let's give them what they desire."

"Oooh brutal," said Zero, "I really like her, but don't get jealous Zee, it's purely platonic." Zendara rolled her eyes and laughed. Mardran set the coordinates before Seventeen could protest any further. They were on course to Feer'aal.

* * * * * * * * * * * * *

The sight of the planet Feer'aal sent shudders down Mardran's spine. So many bad memories, so much pain and buried anger bubbled beneath her calm exterior. Right now, she needed to summon that anger, for it to rise like bile in her throat, to enable her to launch the orbit to terra torpedoes. That single act would alert the Ferrucians to the coming threat, snap them into retaliation, and ultimately lead to their demise. Her finger hovered restlessly above the trigger. Zero-Nine approached her.

"If you wish, I could launch the torpedoes."

"No, it's okay, i'm fine." Mardran's tone wasn't totally convincing.

"I need to do this."

"You do not need to do anything," Zero replied.

"Yes," she said, "I really do, for everything and everyone that they ever took from me... and to ensure that they can never do it again." Her voice had steadied, and before Zero could utter another word, Mardran had pulled the trigger.

"I guess you really did need to do it," said Zero. "Well done."

"Here they come! Right on cue." Zendara

referred to the onrushing Ferrucian fighters that now peppered the scanners. To their rear, The Hound was closing in fast, with Injis's fleet following in its lead.

"Zendara, go dark now."

"Shutting down all non-essential systems," she replied.

"If we don't want to become a very messy sandwich, we need to get out of here," said Zero. He was getting very edgy.

"Mardran, position us in the shadow of the fifth moon," said Seventeen.

"No problem, but what's your plan Seventeen?"

"At the first shot from either side, engage thrusters and shields only, nothing else... and get us out of here at maximum speed. We will use the cover of their fire and preoccupation with obliterating each other, to make our escape."

"What's our heading?"

"Lay in the coordinates for the Broken Crown."

"Ready when you are." The Hope hung in complete blackness, hidden by a backdrop of the dark shadows of the fifth moon.

It began, and as predicted, the Ferrucian fighters commenced firing the second they hit open space.

"Now Mardran," said Seventeen, with a measured calm. The Hope slipped away undetected, as streaks of red blaster fire lit up the void of space. The scarlet bolts from

the Ferrucian canons collided with the bolts
of blue, green and yellow that streaked back
in reply. They looked almost beautiful in
their savagery. The two fleets resembled rival
packs of wild predators that were charging at
each other; fangs and claws bared on a single-
minded mission to kill the other.

Chapter 24 - The Eye

Treelo had witnessed so much over the past few days. Most of which he had previously believed to be made up stories, myths and legends. He had been forced to question his whole concept of reality and his own shallow, self-serving lifestyle. This galaxy held so many secrets, and he wanted to experience more. His eyes and mind had been opened, he had been given no choice but to embrace and respect the unknown, and he was becoming a much better person for it.

He, Lu and Tam moved towards The Eye, and the wall grew taller again. An aperture appeared in the rock and extended outward to form a perfect circle. Legend said that The Eye only opened to those that it had something to show. In ancient times, the Village Elders would stand around the circle religiously. They would fast and wait for The Eye to choose which of them needed to *see*. Back then the messages were practical, mainly related to crops, weather or the threat of invasion by neighbouring villages. Right now The Eye was choosing Lu, Tam and Treelo. It had so much more than practical information to show them. The aperture had made itself wide enough for all three of them to step inside. The trio were instantly immersed in the events that had unfolded in their absence. At first, they were off-balance and disorientated. They soon came to realise that they couldn't affect anything that was happening around them. The three of them looked on helplessly as their friends engaged in battle; they watched in disbelief as The Hunger consumed Fifty-Six, and the sheer scale of Injis's battle fleet, as it emerged from Wild Space. They watched in open-mouthed wonder as Pilots displayed awe-inspiring flying skills in seemingly indestructible ships, neither of which any of them knew Pilots possessed. At least now they knew where Pilot was and that he was safe. They watched as the Slaavene were decimated by Injis's monster fleet, and how they were tracking Seventeen and his crew, who were on a course to Feer'aal.

Then without warning - silence and blackness enveloped them. After a few long seconds, another aperture opened, and a tight beam of light pierced the darkness. It focused on Lu, directly over her heart. She trusted this place now, and after recent events, she felt for the first time that she was truly a child of Veela. She approached the light source and placed her hand inside the aperture. There was something inside, her fingers searched through the dust within the jagged hole. She touched something... it felt like old parchment. Lu removed a small scroll and unrolled it. The scroll illuminated and displayed a map of the Unity. Some of the planets were interlinked; these were the sentient ones, the ancient planets of the Loway routes. The map showed that The Link was what connected the planets to one another. The map highlighted that the Core Loway had been designed and constructed to follow the pathways of The Link.

The Eye was sharing ancient knowledge with them. Unity, Veela VI, Raktar, Lardoria, Pharmora, Tah, the Broken Crown and Home were all visible on the map. Some of them appeared as damaged: where the path of The Link had broken - Feer'aal, Shinara Prime and Slaavene were also present on the map, (displayed as disconnected rogue planets), along with their numerous dark moons, and the Zeta and Wonk'aat asteroid belts.

"This battle is older than we could ever have imagined, and so much vaster." said Lu
A new planet appeared on the map, then vanished as quickly as it had shown up. This action repeated continuously.

"What is it trying to tell us?" asked Treelo.

"I'm not entirely sure," replied Lu. "We are going to need help to figure it out." Vrin knows of many ancient things, she might be able to help. Lu rolled up the scroll and

secured it in the inside pocket of her tunic:
the same pocket that had kept Tecta's
conscious mind safe on her initial journey
from the same planet she now stood upon, once
again.

"Er, guys, how do we get out of here?" It
was as if The Eye had heard Treelo's question.
The aperture reappeared. Lu thanked The Eye
for its insight before they stepped out of the
circle of The Eye, into brilliant sunshine.
"How long were we in there?" asked Treelo,
"Night had only just fallen when we entered."
"Where you go friends?" Pilot's voice
caught them by surprise.
"Pilot! Am I ever glad to see you." Lu
grabbed him and squeezed him tightly.
"Okay, Friend Lu," he laughed. "What
happen here, this dust, now jungle?"
"The Genesis Sphere happened," answered
Tam.
"Wow Friend Tam, you do magic."
"You're the one doing magic in those ships
of yours."
"How you know this things Friend Tam?"
"It's a long story, we'll explain on our
way back to Unity," said Lu, "And Pilot, I am
very sorry about Fifty-Six. We saw you did
everything you could to save him."
"Pilot not forget Friend Fifty-Six. He
make Hornets too."
Treelo hung his head low, he had forgotten how
much Pilot disliked him. He hadn't
acknowledged him at all, and he remembered how

much it actually bothered him. To his
surprise, Pilot approached him and touched his
hand. He gave his best toothy grin and said,

"You different now, you Friend Treelo
now."

"I'll take that," laughed Treelo, then
added, "Thank you, Friend Pilot."

Chapter 25 – The Fall of Feer'aal

"Today is the day of reckoning!" The Chief Elder's coarse voice boomed and echoed around the chamber. "Each and every one of us gathered here has prepared our whole lives for this day, as did our ancestors before us. This day brings us the battle we deserve, and which we have craved, for so long. Today we will honour our forefathers. We shall defend our homes and our sacred way of life. Many of our number may fall in this battle, but it will be a glorious death, a death with meaning! A death worthy of any true Ferrucian. WE WILL BE VICTORIOUS!!"

The pomp and ceremony of this tradition had cost the Ferrucians dearly. For all their talk of preparation, they were totally and utterly unprepared for the ferocity of the attack that had already begun, high above them. Once again, their arrogance and underestimation of the enemy, would be their undoing. Whilst the gathered knelt, heads bowed, wrapt in the archaic rantings of the Elders, the first line of Ferrucian defence was taking an unprecedented battering in the space above Feer'aal. They were too stubborn to call for assistance, even when faced with the unstoppable appetite of The Hunger. They would not accept the glaringly obvious fact that they were losing. They were outnumbered, outgunned and out manoeuvred. Many of the Ferrucian pilots made kamikazee suicide runs in their desperation to save face. They completely depleted their weapons supplies, then followed the last of the weapons they had discharged, on a collision course with the nearest enemy ship. The ship's fuel cells detonated on impact with the enemy vessels, which provided one final opportunity to inflict some damage. The Feruccian pilot's tactics took out a few enemy craft, and inflicted damage on others, but it wasn't enough to turn the tide of the space battle.

While the one-sided dog fight continued to rage in Ferrucian space, a large contingent of Injis's fleet broke away from the battle to descend upon the hellish landscape below. The monstrous wave of craft tore into the cities of Feer'aal like a plague of locusts decimating a crop. The Ferrucian's had put too much faith in their Shrapnel Droids and A.R.K s, that they had deployed as their secondary line of defence. They believed the weapons would afford their warriors the opportunity to prepare for battle in the time-honoured way.

For all their vicious intent and savage design, The Hunger had rendered the weapons useless. The superstitious ceremony delayed the deployment of the ground warriors. They could, (and would not go), into battle until the ceremony was complete. Each warrior had to be anointed with the blood of the ancient ones, before they threw themselves into the fray. For if they fell in battle without performing the ritual, they would never be permitted entry to the dead realm. They would become trapped, helpless spectres. A freshly-anointed horde of warriors had rushed to the defences on the chamber's outer walls. They had been greeted by a devastating sight. The cities of Feer'aal were reduced to lakes of molten rock, metal and fire, under the relentless bombardment of the gigantic enemy ships.

The warriors fired mortars and energy weapons at the approaching craft. More warriors continued to join them, (as and when their ceremonial preparations were complete), but this battle was already lost. The Chamber of Elders was the last bastion of ancient Feer'aal, and it was being crushed. Chunks of ancient stone were blasted from the battlements, which paved the way for the battering ram of ships to smash their way through. The decimated chamber, and every soul gathered within, were crushed. The ramming vessels continued to crush and push until the chamber buildings, (and all those who had

perished inside), were swallowed into the
fiery abyss of the Kraqtar Ravine.

The space battle was over, and Injis's fleet
had been marginally thinned. From orbit, she
and Vrex observed the absolute carnage that
was being wrought on the surface.

"This battle bores me Vrex. Instruct the
fleet to finish it. Once it is done, they are
to regroup and await orders on the edge of
Unity space.

"As you wish. Where are we going?"

"We have an errand to run." The Vengeance
broke its orbit and headed to Unity.

Chapter 26 - Inside

The Hope set down in the familiar cave on BC1215 in the Broken Crown. This had been the vessel's home for many years. Up until the quest for the Unity Spire and the arrival of the Siblings, the Protectors had been incarcerated on the cavernous rock, with little hope of ever leaving.

Zero-Nine alighted The Hope first. Taire and Vrin were there to greet them. In true Taire fashion, he had wasted no time in getting to work on the diamond-shielding, and couldn't wait to show Seventeen his progress so far. Vrin took Zendara and Mardran through to an adjacent cave, where a makeshift kitchen of sorts, had been fashioned. They looked in dire need of some sustenance and rest.

"I have studied the spec of Pilot's Hornet. Its shielding is a masterpiece of pure genius in engineering. Fifty-Six certainly knew his way around an engine too, and as for that nose drill..."

"Taire, sorry to be blunt, but can you modify it to make it work on us, or not?" Seventeen knew he had to interrupt, before Taire meandered off into total tech-nerd territory.

"You're right, apologies friends. I have modified the shield so it works in a similar way to our combat suits. However, because of the vast amounts of power needed to generate the diamond-shielding, unlike our combat suits, they cannot be permanently activated. Instead, your new shielding will auto-armour any area of impact from conventional weapons or physical force. More importantly, in the presence of The Hunger, it will activate total defence systems - making you completely impenetrable."

"Boring, just suit me up already," said Zero-Nine.

"Patience Zero-Nine," snapped Seventeen. "Thank you Taire, that was very thorough. Are you ready to apply the technology? More importantly, will it work?" In spite of snapping at Zero, Seventeen sounded a little impatient himself.

"The science is sound..."

"Taire, I am sensing a *but*."

"You're right Seventeen. I can't lie. The problem I've had is that I only had the readings from Pilot's shield log to work from. I don't have an actual specimen of The Hunger to test it. Also, I only have enough for the two of you. The rest is needed to shield the fleet."

"We will just have to have faith then. There is no time to waste." Seventeen was being pragmatic, rather than a martyr.

"Okay, Seventeen, are you going to go first?" asked Taire.

"Yes, I am ready." Taire opened Seventeen's access panel and inserted the shield tech.

"There, it is done."

"Is that it?" said Seventeen.

"Yes, that is *actually* it," replied Taire.

"How will we know if it works?" Zero-Nine swung a fist at Seventeen's head, his arm ricocheted off the shielding.

"It works!" exclaimed Zero-Nine.

"So, I am impenetrable?" asked Seventeen.

"You said it," laughed Zero.   "Don't be so hard on yourself Seventeen, I'm sure there's someone out there who would find you attractive enough to want to penetrate you. Although I had you down as more of a pitcher than a receiver... but hey, each to their own!"

"Zero-Nine, cease your inane ramblings and get your shielding installed. While you are at it Taire, could you possibly disable his vocal processors?"

"Seventeen, did you just make an actual joke? Ha ha ha… actually, you were making a serious request, weren't you?" Taire laughed discreetly, but Seventeen remained silent, and enjoyed his moment in quiet contentment.

* * * * * * * * * *

Lu, Tam, Pilot and Treelo alighted the Loway pod inside the cave. Tecta was waiting with Gliis and several scared Unitians. Taire, Zero-Nine and Seventeen were in The Hope, and all the other evacuees were stowed safely throughout the Broken Crown. Each Protector had been assigned a group to watch over until any threat had past.

"She is here, and she has come alone," came Tecta's voice through the comms.

"She must have broken off from the battle, the rest of her fleet were fully engaged when we slipped away," Seventeen responded.

"She's bold, I'll give her that," added Lu.

"No Lu, she is reckless and arrogant. Her weapon has made her believe she is unbeatable, and until Taire gets the diamond- shielding perfected, her belief, sadly, is justified." said Seventeen.

"We cannot just sit here, she could destroy everything we have started to build. I will not hide away and let her do this."

"Lu, that is exactly what you must do. I have seen her type before. She is child-like in her need for instant gratification. When she finds the planet is empty, she will tire of it quickly, and be on her way. We will not move against her until we know that we have a fighting chance of defeating her. As for destroying the new Unity, we are more than a collection of planets and physical structures.

We are a people; and a strong resilient people at that." said Tecta

"Her fleet won't be far behind her," added Seventeen.

"And Tecta is right Lu, she would not have come here without her weapon aboard that ship. We can't move against her yet."

"What happened to 'I am impenetrable?'" sniped Zero.

"We do need to test the shielding before you go running headlong into battle. I have seen what her weapon does. The surveillance recording from Pilot's Hornet showed what happened to Fifty-Six... it was devastating." It was fair to say Taire was more than a little bit nervous about sending his friends into battle with experimental armour of his design. Their lives were literally in the hands of his work.

Chapter 27 – Broken Hope

The Vengeance slipped unchallenged through the asteroids and debris of the Broken Crown. Onward through Unity's atmosphere and down to the surface: they met no resistance, no defences of any kind. Unity had become a ghost planet. The Vengeance made a velvet-soft landing at the crest of a mountain range; the same mountain range that had been the setting for the Endless War. Injis stepped from her pristine ship, the only sound that greeted her was the hum of thrusters powering down, and the late evening breeze as it whipped about the Unity Spire. Vrex accompanied her in his ever-grovelling manner.

"Where are the mighty Protectors?" shouted Injis, as if they were hiding in ear shot. All she was met with were the echoes of her own question, which returned to her from the vacuous gaps in the mountain range.

"Tell me Vrex, do you suppose that they have fled, like rodents, scurrying from the flood that is my power?" She came to realise her goading was useless, she would get no reaction. There was no one ~~here~~ around to hear her scathing words.

"Surely this is the case, my fearsome leader."

"So, they have left their precious planet, alone and vulnerable, in the dark. You could say without *protection*, how ironic." She did the closest thing to a laugh that she was capable of.

"What a crushing disappointment this is," she sighed at length. "For now, I will let them run and hide. Eventually, they will all bow before me, or be healed. As for the Protectors, The Hunger will erase all traces of their existence from the galaxy." There was a slight pause as Injis' mind ticked over. "As we are here, unopposed, another opportunity has presented itself. I can put an end to any fantastical notions of a Unity Spire that can save them." Injis approached the spire in menacingly slow steps, as if trying to intimidate the rock itself. "The Hushed were weak in their physical form. I, however, am not. No outdated relic will stand in my way."

Injis stood before the Unity Spire, she eyed it with disdain.

"What an unremarkably bland, ugly rock. Vrex, let's lighten it up." The cyan fire in her eyes intensified, it blazed wildly like a raging bush fire in the depths of the night. She raised her porcelain white arms; their fragile appearance belied the raw power that surged within her. She extended her slender fingers and channelled her most intense fire. Cyan flames blasted from her fingertips, and engulfed the slate-black column of rock. The flames penetrated the dense structure, until it glowed with the cyan blue of Injis's fire.

"Now Vrex, smash it." Vrex lifted his pulse hammer, drew it back, and swung like a steroid-fuelled executioner. The weapon collided with the rocky surface and unleashed the pulse surge. The energy of the surge penetrated deep into the Spire, where it concentrated and charged. The Spire shuddered and creaked, then it exploded from the inside out, like a heated corn kernel. It was completely obliterated by the pulse surge. Shards of rock were propelled high into the night sky, then like a vicious rain, the splintered fragments showered back down, piercing the ground all around them.

"That's such an improvement, don't you think?"

"Indeed it is, my talented leader, you are quite the artist."

The fragments of the Spire protruded from the ground, like a bed of shiny nails. They glistened in the moonlight. Injis sighed with satisfaction, and looked up to the heavens.

"Ahhh my most beautiful creation. I had almost forgotten what a marvel you are to behold. Vrex, this is where my true journey began." She was too blinded by the Broken Crown's beauty to even consider that her enemies had taken refuge within.

"Once again, you astound me with your brilliance," he grovelled.

"Sometimes Vrex, you are quite the sycophant, but I like that about you. Come, there is no fight to be had here. We will return to Exhilar. Order the fleet to return also. We shall await the futile attempts of retaliation that the Protectors are undoubtedly dreaming up."

Chapter 28 - The Healer?

One day before the self-imposed exile of The Mora.

The Instrument was complete. Hours upon hours of meticulous testing and research had led to this moment. Injis had chosen her test subject well. The moon Juwel, was populated by a sickly, disease-ridden people, and that disease was called mortality. She was ready to heal them all. She ran a final diagnostic on The Instrument. Surgical laser scalpels were precision tools; effective, but so small and limited. Injis had taken it upon herself to upscale and perfect the tool, and now came the moment of truth.

Injis chose to test her creation well away from her own world. She had convinced herself that these were the optimum test conditions. She had loaded The Instrument onto a research craft, and locked it in a protracted orbit around Shinara Prime. Injis locked on to Juwel's coordinates and charged The Instrument to maximum power. Her slim, white finger was poised over the activation pad. The lock tone chimed, she exhaled from the depths of her being, and pushed the button.

"You are healed," she whispered. The laser scalpel burned through the moon's atmosphere, then its crust: the beam bored deep into Juwel's core. The moon's core temperature rose to critical levels. Within minutes, the crust could not contain the molten furnace that raged within; and with an almighty CRACK - Juwel ripped itself wide open, and exploded in a blaze of molten rock and fire.

"You are welcome," whispered Injis, as she powered down her instrument of mass healing. Injis was filled with pride on her journey back to Pharmora. She couldn't wait to tell The Elders of the great healing she had performed. They would be so proud of her achievements. The child prodigy had come of age, at just ten years old.

Back on Pharmora, Injis presented her work to The Elders. They didn't see her triumph in the same warped way that she did.

"What is wrong with you child? This is not the Mora way. You have committed an act of genocide," fumed the chief elder, Janlis.

"There is nothing wrong with me. I represent what The Mora are meant to be."

"My child, you have become unwell, and you have been misguided. You must allow us to help you." Injis continued to argue as she was escorted to a secure treatment chamber.

"I do not need to be fixed, I am fulfilling our destiny. We are meant to heal the universe."

"Healing and killing are two very different things," said one of her escorts sternly, as they released her into the chamber.

"I'm offering a permanent solution: to end the sickness and suffering of mortals. The ultimate cure." Her ravings were silenced by the chemical-infused mist that flooded the reinforced glass chamber. Two Mora entered the chamber, and wore pristine white chem suits to shield them from the mist. They secured her limbs, and strapped her head to the steel surgical table. Her fire had dulled from a rage-fuelled roar, to a faint smoulder. Although it felt like it, this wasn't a cell, it was a treatment room. The real cell was Injis's own mind... into which she had receded, arguing and protesting to herself.

Unbeknownst to The Elders, Injis's flame had been infiltrated by the black smoke of The Hushed. She had been tricked. She'd bargained White Rock for knowledge, in her quest to heal. However, there was no knowledge, just very bad advice, and black smoke corrupted her flame. In that one act, she had naively created two monsters. The Hushed now possessed the telepathic abilities of the sacred White Rock. It had enabled them to affect the thoughts, feelings and actions of the people of our realm, from the phase realm. The second was the thing that she herself had become. The Mora were the product of a symbiotic relationship between the Flame of Mora, and the telepathic White Rock. Each Mora's flame or soul originated from the Flame of Mora, and Injis had allowed her soul to be infiltrated by The Hushed. The soul chose a form for itself, which was forged from the White Rock. Most Mora chose practicality; multiple limbs and brains to enhance medical and surgical expertise. There was no scope for vanity. Aesthetic appearance was of no consequence. Some Mora looked cumbersome, ridiculous even, but it was all in the name of furthering their craft. Injis's corrupted flame had chosen a seductive humanoid form, created to make herself relatable to the peoples of the galaxy that she had already chosen to make it her mission to heal.

Injis had to be contained. The Mora needed to learn how this monster had come to be. They felt that it was their responsibility to ensure that a tragedy, such as the Juwel massacre, was never allowed to happen again. They locked the Flame of Mora, and left their home planet of Pharmora. They vowed never to allow another of their kind to be created, until they found a way to cure Injis, and prevent any further corruption of the flame.

Chapter 29 – Coming of Age

"She is leaving." Tecta had been watching and waiting anxiously for Injis to depart the planet.

"Now can we go home?" asked Lu.

"Once she has cleared Unity space."

"Thank you, Tecta, for stopping me before, I was emotional and impulsive."

"I would expect nothing else Lu. You are true to your nature, and I would never want to change that. Well, maybe I'd add a small pinch of patience." Lu hugged Tecta, and squeezed him tightly.

"We need a plan. Gliis, Taire and I will go to the Unity Spire. There must be some wisdom we can glean from it."

"Very well, I will gather our people in the Houses of Unity, and await your return," Tecta replied.

* * * * * * * * * *

Lu stood over the vicious shards of black slate rock. The fragile looking pieces littered the whole area where The Unity Spire had stood.

"There must be more than a million pieces," said Taire sadly. "Even I can't fix this. What do we do now Lu?"

"I....I....really don't know Brother."

"She is here," said Gliis. Up to this point, he hadn't uttered a word.

"Lu, Taire." They looked up from the rock-strewn floor. There before them was Etala's essence stood before them all. She sparkled like a sea of precious gems in humanoid form.

"Why such despair, my children? It was never about the physical object that was The Unity Spire. It was, and still is, about the three of you; focusing your energy and working together, in the belief that you can change the galaxy for the better. You have surpassed yourselves in your efforts so far. The real power comes from within you, you do not need an ancient relic to wield it. It is written in your DNA, your minds and your very souls. The Spire was merely a tool to channel your belief, and enable you to unleash your full potential. You were born for this purpose. You must learn to use your gifts, control your powers, and if you truly believe, then anything is possible. Now my children, fix the Unity Spire.

"But you said it didn't matter," said Nataalu, a little confused.

"The Spire doesn't matter. What does matter is that you can fix it."

"How?" asked Gliis.

"There is not a right or wrong way, trust each other. Remember how you felt when *you* activated the Liberty Spike, that connection, that energy, it lives within the three of you."

Lu, Taire and Gliis cast their minds back to the events inside the Liberty Chamber seep within The Silence. They stood in the same positions that they had taken up on that day. Lu extended her arms out in front of her, palms facing down, and closed her eyes. Taire and Gliis followed her lead.

"Now breathe deeply - down into your core," said Etala. "Visualise the Spire in your mind's eye. Try to recall the minutia, every tiny detail. Imagine it, complete. The Siblings felt the connection passing through them. It was a calming, yet powerful, sensation. Shards of the shattered rock started to quiver and hover above the ground, moving towards each other, as if being manipulated by magnetic attraction. The Siblings moved their arms outward in unison. Without saying a word, they instinctively tilted their palms to face each other's. The shards spun collectively within the boundaries of the triangle that the Siblings had formed. The tiny pieces created a stone cyclone. They locked together, as they whipped around with ever increasing velocity. The Siblings opened their eyes in perfect synchronicity, and the Unity Spire stood before them... completely restored. The Siblings smiled at each other, breathlessly.

"Children, you are more remarkable than you know. You have achieved something that many would deem impossible. Individually, your gifts are strong, but when they are joined, your combined power is immense. Use your gifts wisely for the greater good," smiled Etala.

"Mother, The Eye of Veela gave this to me." Lu reached inside the folds of her tunic and produced the scroll. She unrolled it to show Etala the map. Etala cast her ethereal hand over the image on the scroll; the glyphs that represented the planets shifted position, leaving a blank circular space in the centre of the parchment. Four basic stick figures appeared in the space.

"The Eye opened to you?"

"Yes, to Tam, Treelo and Me."

"Mother, who are the people on the scroll? They were not there before," asked Gliis.

"They are the three of you."

"How can they be us? That scroll looks ancient, we were not even thought of when it was made." Taire's logical brain had taken over.

"My children, your ascension is well documented in ancient legend and folklore across the galaxy, though the stories have been largely forgotten. Since you led the victory over The Hushed, the stories have resurfaced. The galaxy is starting to believe once again."

"Why have you not told any of us about

this before? And why are there four figures on the map?" Lu was shaken by what she had just heard.

"These matters are delicate, and you have now proven yourselves ready to hear the information I am about to share with you."

"Two more children of The Unity have awoken. One more awaits the awakening. They will make allies of the highest calibre. I see that you, Nataalu, have found one of them already."

"Tam," exclaimed Lu, with a beaming smile.

"Your instincts serve you well my child."

"What if we cannot find the other two?" asked Gliis

"Gliis, you are already closer than you know, and Taire - you must look deep inside yourself to find the sixth. I cannot tell you anymore than this, these discoveries must be made on your own, in your own time. Know that you can still win this battle for The Unity, with or without these allies. However, you will need all three to overcome the future challenges that await you in the quest for peace.

Now you must journey to Exhilar. You will each know the part you must play once you get there. Trust yourselves, and your gifts."

The sun peered over the horizon and Etala's smiling essence faded away. A new day had dawned, and the Siblings had a renewed sense of purpose and belief: they felt ready to face whatever awaited them.

Chapter 30 - Plan of attack

The mid-afternoon sun shone down upon the Houses of Unity. Tecta and Seventeen grew impatient, they had been waiting in the corridors for what seemed like hours.

"Tecta, it is the duty of us all to protect the Siblings. You have already laid down your life more than once," said Seventeen, adamant in his tone.

"And you my friend, gifted me another chance at life."

"And I will not let you risk it so brazenly again."

"This argument is null and void Seventeen. You and Zero-Nine have already been fitted with the diamond-shielding, have you not?"

"So, you will both join the ground assault. Take good care of my children."

"Of course old friend, and you take care of my ship and crew."

"You can stop talking about me now," said Zero-Nine, as he approached with the Siblings.

"Wrong. We were discussing strategies, something you wouldn't know much about." said

Seventeen
    "Oh, ha ha, leave the comedy to me,"
replied Zero-Nine. Tecta gave the Siblings a
knowing nod.

The remainder of the council members had
already taken their seats in the chamber when
the Siblings and Protectors entered.
    "Greetings friends and allies," Lu
addressed the gathered.
    "Before we begin to speak of strategy,
Pilot has a disturbing, but vital,
surveillance clip that we all need to see. We
need to understand the gravity of the
situation we are in, and what we are up
against. When you are ready Pilot." Pilot's
toothy grin was absent; he had no wish to
inflict the images on anyone, let alone watch
it himself again, but he knew he must. Pilot
showed the footage of Fifty-Six's demise on
the chamber's main holoscreen. The images left
every soul in the chamber in stunned silence.
    "Thank you, Pilot." Lu placed a reassuring
hand on Pilot's shoulder. "We will not force
anyone to fight, but I will say, we are going
to need all the help we can get to save the
Unity. Who will stand with us in this battle?"
    "We will stand with you," Targole
responded first, almost instantaneously, much
to Lu's surprise.
    "After the sacrifice we have just
witnessed, we cannot stand by and do nothing."
    "We are with you," the entire council
delegation agreed, who echoed Targole's

sentiment.

"Thank you, my friends," smiled Lu.

"We are not unprepared for this fight," said Taire, who stood and addressed the chamber. "We have modified weaponry that will not be vulnerable to the metal-eating substance that the enemy depends heavily upon. Targole, we have constructed carbon-fibre shields and electro-pikes - for you and your warriors. I know these are your preferred weapons."

"Thank you, my friend," smiled Targole.

"We have also fashioned blasters, body armour and energy blade hilts from the same substance, for all who wish to take up arms." The council members nodded in appreciation.

"We do have a plan of attack," said Lu. "Ground troops will be transported to Exhilar on the Core Loway. Taire and I will lead the ground assault on the mountains edge, shown on Pilot's footage. Targole, you and your warriors will engage the Scavenger army on the flats. When we have won our respective battles, we will rendezvous at the Black Palace. Pilots will leave the surface in their Hornet's to join the fleet in Exhilar space. The fleet will be led by Tecta, Zendara and Mardran. Seventeen and Zero-Nine, your primary objective is to ensure that no enemy troops gain access to the subterranean cave system. This is where Gliis will be returning the White Rock to the keepers of the flame. If the visions shown to him by The Link are accurate, then it is key to our strategy and survival that his mission is successful. Please make your preparations, we leave in three hours. For peace!"

"For peace!" boomed the unified voices of the council that filled the chamber.

Tecta approached Lu.

"Nataalu, come walk with me." Tecta sounded serious, he only used Lu's full name when he was being serious. He led her outside into the cool evening air. Many hours had passed in the council chambers, and the short autumnal day had already drawn to a close.

"Look around us Nataalu, this place is a beacon of shining hope in the darkness." Lu regarded the groups of different species that sat around small fires sharing food, drink and stories. Some sang and danced as varied exotic aromas filled their senses. Hope thrived here, and chatting and merriment coloured the air. The atmosphere was more that of a festival than the eve of war. "Now Nataalu, look up above us." The sky was majestically clear, peppered with billions of brilliant stars.

"Each of those shimmering lights represents another potential beacon of hope. Never lose sight of what it is that we are fighting for Nataalu. All that we do must be in the best interests of The Unity. In our endeavours to fulfil this quest, we must never lose ourselves in the fight."

"I think I understand Tecta, but why are you telling me this now?"

"I fear I have overstepped the mark, and

lost some part of myself to the fight. While you were on Veela VI, I ordered Seventeen to lead Injis's fleet to Feer'aal and attack the planet. I did this to use the Feruccian's certain retaliation as a weapon for our own ends, to buy us some time. Now I fear that Feer'aal will not survive the global assault Injis's fleet has inflicted. I will have to make my own peace with my actions when this conflict is over. We are on the eve of another battle, and I never want you to be in the regrettable position I have put myself in."

"You acted in the best interest of The Unity. I will not judge you for giving us a fighting chance."

"At what cost? Promise me you will remember what we have spoken of here today, and never repeat the mistakes that I have made."

"As always, I treasure your wisdom and guidance Tecta," said Lu, who regarded him quizzically. Something about his manner reminded her of their final hours on Veela VI, and it didn't sit comfortably. She placed her hand on his shoulder.

"We saw Etala's essence at the Unity Spire. Injis had destroyed the Spire, shattered it. Taire, Gliis and I used our gifts to restore it, under Etala's guidance. There is so much we don't yet know, but Etala has assured us that we can win this battle. There is so much more to tell, and we will need your guidance more than ever going forward. What happens next is key, and we will succeed today, together."

Chapter 31 - Exhilar

"Soon The Unity will bring their futile attack. They will be no match for me, or any of you. The Hunger will destroy the Protector Droids, taking them out of the equation. Without them, the rest are nothing but a ramshackle ensemble of pitiful mortals. We will be victorious on this day. We will take this galaxy for our own. My fleet is armed, and ready to bring destruction to any threats from above. Are you, my warriors, ready to destroy our enemies on the ground?" The Gantuans and Scavengers knelt in salute.

"Yes leader," they grunted in unison.

"I can't hear you," she hissed. "Let's hear it with some fire in your bellies, or I will give you some fire of my own. ARE YOU READY TO FIGHT?!!" Injis shouted.

"YES LEADER!" the troops roared.

"That's better, now take up your positions. The second they rear their ugly heads… blow them off!"

The Scavengers took up infantry positions

between the Black Palace and the caves, whilst the Gantuans took their positions on the higher ground, amongst the rocks and ledges. Injis and Vrex retreated to the battlements of the Black Palace; the perfect spot to watch their coming victory unfold.

"Vrex, once we have finished with this minor annoyance, and gathered the remaining White Rocks, we will complete our objective; and give life to a new, more ruthless, generation of Mora."

"Your brilliance knows no bounds my Leader."

"You always know the right thing to say Vrex. I may even treat you to a vial of Micro Droids when this battle is done. Your skin isn't as raw as I know you like it." Vrex wore a perverse smile, and bowed his head.

Chapter 32 - Above Exhilar Part 1

The Hope led the fleet into Exhilar space. Injis's fleet lay menacingly in wait, the battle on Feer'aal had thinned their number a little, but her armada was still substantial and deadly. The Unity fleet was small, but equally deadly, made up of small, well-equipped fighters, piloted by the best the Unity had to offer. Mardran was just one such example.

"Tecta, we have incoming transmissions," said Zendara.

"Okay, on screen."

"Protector Droid! I am Chandira of Feer'aal." The Feruccian that spoke was young, clearly inexperienced, and angry too, but devoid of any battle scars.

"We are what remains of our people's warriors, and we seek to destroy our mutual enemy. Our homeworld is decimated, our families murdered and our homes nothing more than dust. We demand revenge."

"If you are here on a suicide mission of

vengeance, then you fight alone. If you are here to fight for the Unity and preserve both our ways of life, then we will fight for our futures together." Tecta was all too aware of the hypocrisy that laced his self-righteous words.

"We will call it solidarity if this pleases you," came the Feruccian's reply.

"On this day, I will accept this reasoning. Together we can succeed, but you need to listen to me. The enemy possess a weapon which you cannot defend against. It eats through metal. We have developed defensive shielding to protect against it. Your covering fire would be much appreciated, and it is much needed."

"This is an insult, you mean to steal our glory and deny us our vengeance. We are strong, and we will not…" Tecta ended the transmission.

"Tecta, we have another incoming transmission." said Mardran

"Okay, open comms," he sighed.

"This is Captain Raxnelle, of the Slaavene command ship Marauder. We come to fight with you, to honour our fallen."

"Slaavene, we welcome your assistance. As you well know, the enemy has a metal-eating weapon. We are now shielded against this weapon. Your ships are not. We will not put you in the face of inevitable death. If you wish to fight with us, then we would welcome some much needed covering fire. I am not in a position to command you, but I would ask that you stay well back."

"We understand. We will assist in any way that we can, to honour our brethren."

"We appreciate your help and understanding, thank you."

"NO!" screamed Tecta over open comms. The Feruccians had charged at full thrust ahead of the Unity fleet, their lasers and missiles blazed. Despite the small dent they had made in the enemy fleet, they were ended in seconds by The Hunger.

"Tecta to Unity fleet. Hold your nerve. The Feruccians have made a fatal mistake, despite our warnings to use caution. Clear this from your minds. We are shielded, we will imminently engage the enemy. Remember your training, trust your instincts and remember what it is that we fight for: The Unity, our way of life, and our future peace. Slaavene fleet, you are with us now, we will forge a path ahead together."

The welcome sight of the Hornets broke through Exhilar's atmosphere. The fleet's hearts were filled with some much-needed hope, and it was the cue to engage Injis's fleet.

"Unity fleet, full attack speed now! Follow Pilot's ships and exploit the breaches they make. Slaavene fleet, concentrate as much fire upon their lead ships as you can."
Once again, Pilots ripped hole after hole in the enemy vessels. The small, manoeuvrable ships of the Unity fleet followed the Hornets,

and inflicted fatal blows on the enemy ships, from the inside. It was as simple as threading a needle. They weaved a deadly tapestry throughout the entirety of the enemy fleet, carving them to pieces. The Hunger was deployed again and again, to no effect. Yet still they launched it like madmen, repeating a futile exercise in the vain hope of a different outcome. The nimble craft were an impossible target for the monstrous ships of Injis's fleet.

"So, size does matter," laughed Zee. "Just not in the way the old saying suggests."

"Zendara, I believe you may have been spending too much time with Zero-Nine." Tecta's tone was devoid of humour, but Mardran couldn't suppress a smirk. The Hunger had proven ineffective on the Unity ships, and the frustration of having zero defences against the Hornets drove several of Injis's ships to fall back, and retreat to the depths of Wild Space. The armada that remained was still formidable, and they had a last-ditch plan. The remaining ships interlocked to form a battering ram formation, the same one they had used to wipe the cities of Feer'aal clean off the face of the planet. The newly- formed battering ram switched to conventional weapons. They spat laser blasts and torpedoes as they drew ever closer to the Unity vessels. A few took hits, but the diamond-shielding was robust enough to render the effects of the weapon's impacts superficial. The combination of the Hornets that continued to punch holes, and the Unity ships that exploited those holes, coupled with the heavy bombardment from the Slaavene fleet, slowed the mobile megastructure. There was, however, one problem. The Hornet's power cells had depleted fast.

"Friend Tecta, Pilots need go, recharge."

"Understood Pilot, we will hold them off for as long as we can. Hurry back!"

"Good luck Friends," said Pilot, as he reluctantly led the Hornets back to the Core Loway. The battering ram continued to move imposingly toward the fleet, it gathered momentum as it went.

"Marauder, hit them hard, then retreat to a safer distance. They are getting too close," barked Tecta. He didn't want any more deaths on his hands, unless they were those of the enemy.

"Understood, it has been an honour to fight with alongside you," said Raxnelle, solemnly.

"The honour is all ours," replied Tecta.

Chapter 33 - Ground assault

Lu and Taire were the first to emerge from the darkness of the cave system . They burst out into the bright orange haze of Exhilar's sunlight. They were flanked by the awe-inspiring forms of Seventeen and Zero-Nine, who took their positions either side of the cave entrance. Tam and Treelo followed, heads held high in full-fitted, black, carbon- fibre armour.

More than a few of the Scavengers turned and ran in complete panic at the first sight of Seventeen and Zero-Nine. They tore away from the group, but there was no escape; only the Black Palace loomed ahead of them, it blocked their retreat. A furious Injis screamed from the battlements. She whipped her hand in a ferocious circular motion above her head, as if wielding an invisible lasso. In this scenario, the Scavengers were her unruly cattle that needed to be brought under control. Injis clenched her fist... the treacherous Scavengers froze, and levitated a

few inches from the ground. Injis displayed
the exact same power she had used on Shrimp,
so many years before. Their bodies were arched
and rigid, arms and heads thrown back, the
mark of the flame on their necks burned almost
as intensely as the cyan fire in their hollow
eyes. She pointed a slender white finger,
singling out one of their number. She intended
to make a big impression. Injis curled her
finger towards herself, and beckoned the
Scavenger to come to her. He floated eerily up
to the battlements. Once he was within
striking distance, she delivered a savage blow
to his head. A sickening thump, crack and
squelch sounded, as Injis's stone fist sank
into the top of his head. The force was so
violent, it created enough pressure to push
his eyes from their sockets.

"Cowards!" screamed Injis. "I command you
to fight, or suffer the same fate as your
cracked-egg-like friend here."

The Scavengers involuntarily responded with
immediate effect - they went on the attack
like a pack of snarling, rabid animals, on a
collision course with the Unitians. The
Unitian's, lead by Lu and Taire, peeled away
towards the mountainous terrain that flanked
the battlefield. As they divided, they
revealed the onrushing R'aal horde; they were
a sea of screaming barbarians. Targole was the
spearhead of his people's attack. They engaged
the Scavengers with a crash and clank of
blades and spears. It was a throwback to the

battles of ancient times - unadulterated hand-to-hand brutality. The images of Fifty-Six's demise, and the distress of Pilots as they rushed helplessly to his aid, spurred Targole on. It fuelled his bubbling rage, and had been strong enough to transform his initial reluctance into pure defiance. He was leading his people to defend The Unity. They charged onwards, electropikes raised, cutting through the Scavenger warriors: they would not fail. The R'aal's prowess with a shield and pike was majestic; ancient combat techniques coupled with devastating technology. It was the most beautiful art form of savagery to behold. They leapt, spun and flipped like deadly acrobats.

Meanwhile, Lu and Taire fanned their troops and eased their way into the rocky outcrops. They were bringing a very different type of fight to the Gantuans. The Unitians had the advantage - the years spent locked in the Endless War had prepared them well for this exact situation. They were used to full on guerilla warfare, and the Gantuans, armed with only laser whips and overconfidence, were at a massive disadvantage. Those whips could rip limbs and heads from torsos with a single stroke, but they had to get close enough to use them. The solid, reptilian, physique and the thick skin of the Gantuans, made the prospect of victory in toe-to-toe combat highly unlikely. The key to winning this fight was distance, cover and projectile weaponry. The wave of Unity fighters wove their way through the rocky outcrops, zigging and zagging, as they launched volley after volley of pulse and frag grenades and spat sporadic bursts of blaster fire, spraying energy bolts in wide arcs. There was nowhere for the Gantuans to hide. They were forced into a full frontal attack. They charged from the cover of the rocks. It was a total berserker move. The Unitians cut them down as they charged. The terrifying threat of the blood-thirsty reptilian juggernauts didn't faze them, despite each of them weighing more than a tonne and running straight at them. The fighters stood their ground and stuck to the plan. Flush them out and mow them down. The Gantuans did not go down without a fight; several of the Unity fighters were relieved of their heads and limbs. They were wrenched from their bodies by the vicious lashes of the laser whips. Any fighters who were exposed and unfortunate enough to find themselves within the reptilian's whip range, were already dead. They had suffered losses, but ultimately the victory belonged to the Unity fighters.

Taire's technical mind had been working overtime, dissecting how Injis had such powerful control over the Scavengers. He surmised that she must be using some kind of remote signal to control them. He concluded that this was nothing more than smoke and mirrors, tech dressed up to look like other-worldly power.

    "Zero, can you scan the area and isolate

any remote signals in the vicinity of Injis, or the Scavengers?"

"I'm on it like a nose cone on a Hornet. Sending scan data now."

"That's impressive, thanks Zero. Maybe work on the jokes though."

"What can I say? It's a gift, and humour is subjective. Maybe you just don't get me," said Zero cockily. Taire had stopped listening. He was totally absorbed in the data feed.

"Lu, I need more time to study the data Zero is sending, can you distract Injis?"

"On my way." Lu engaged full combat mode and headed for the palace.

"Ha!" Injis forced out a monosyllabic cackle, "You have no idea who or what you are dealing with!" She projected her voice over the violence. "Goodbye Protector Droids, unleash The Hunger!" Two missiles blasted from The Vengeance, which was stationed on top of the Black Palace. The warheads raced through the carnage and mess of blaster bolts on the battlefield - the pair of missiles swerved and weaved intelligently towards Seventeen and Zero-Nine.

"Hey, 'The Hunger,' welcome to the inedible," laughed Zero.

"Zero, will you shut up you idiot! We don't even know if this shielding works properly."

"We don't? Kl'aat dung! Excuse me, 'The Hunger', just in case you were listening, I suggest you try my friend as an aperitif. He's number seventeen on the menu."

"Zero-Nine, I swear if they don't eat you, I'll kill you and eat you myself."

"Really Seventeen, there's no need to be such a... Seventeen, but don't worry we can work on your anger management issues later"

"Just brace yourself!" commanded Seventeen. The two Protectors took up defensive stances, and waited for the precise moment. The diamond-shielding activated, it completely encased them in an armoured second skin.

"Wow!" exclaimed Zero-Nine.

"Now!" screamed Seventeen. He side-stepped to evade the missile, and slammed his fist into the body of the incoming weapon. Simultaneously, Zero-Nine thrust a leg forward, his foot collided head on with the nose of the warhead. It relented under the force of the impact, its casing crumpled, but that didn't stop it from deploying its payload. Both weapons spat The Hunger, and covered the two droids. This was the moment of truth.

"Hey! Injis!" Lu shouted up at her from the steps of the palace. Injis glared down at her with pure disdain.

"Oh, dear mortals, you pitiful sacks of meat and water. You send a child to confront me?"

"I am Nataalu. The last person that uttered those words to me met a grisly end, as will you."

"Oh so young and bold, full of hope and aspiration. Yet your feeble form will never allow you the time to meet your full potential. Born with an undetermined, yet inevitable, expiration date. Well, today is that expiration date."

"How about you bring that mouth down here so I can shut it for you."

"Vrex, deal with this child, would you? Don't rush it though. Play with her a little. Children like to play, and she deserves a little fun for her boldness." Vrex leapt from the battlements, and smashed his pulse hammer into the volcanic ground. Lu opened fire, but the tremor caused by Vrex's hammer blow knocked her off-balance, and jolted her aim. As Lu got back to her feet, Injis continued her damning narrative. She ranted relentlessly ~~on~~ about the failings of mortals.

"So fragile... you slowly grow into such warm, smooth, supple and beautiful forms. But to what end? Gravity takes the best parts of you. It's weight, coupled with the passage of time, drags your weak flesh toward the ground. What was once pert and beautiful - becomes heavy; sagging like molten plastic in extreme slow motion, until you are dried up and dead - like so much insignificant dust in the wind."

Injis was so wrapped up in her self-fulfilling bragging, that she had failed to notice that Lu was holding her own against Vrex, and she had gained a reinforcement in the form of

Targole. He had fought his way through Injis's horde of mindless puppets to stand fearlessly by Lu's side.

"I've got this Lu, you get up there and end her." Lu pushed off hard from the ground and engaged Zero G mode. She powered up to the battlements, and landed silently behind Injis.

"Hey!" she shouted, "You know nothing of beauty or strength. It lies within. You will never understand the complexities of the mortal form, the immortal soul, or the things that come with them - love, pride, empathy." Lu was trying to buy Taire as much time as possible.

"I know plenty about the mortal body, and the immortal soul. I have healed many over the millennia, freed them from their pathetic existence, incarcerated in their weak fleshy shells." She hurled a bolt of cyan fire at Lu, but she stood firm and unflinching, and trusted her combat suit to absorb the impact. Injis did her best to hide her surprise, and resumed her rhetoric.

"As for beauty, do you find your shattered moon Juwel to be beautiful? I was born of this galaxy, and I single-handedly created that beautiful phenomenon. I set that whole moon full of immortal souls free from their fragile casings. I healed them. Now they have no more worry of suffering or disease."

Lu tried to subdue her anger, but her fingers twitched restlessly. She drew her twin blades and took up a defensive stance.

"You will pay for every life you have taken."

"Oh child, what do you plan to do with those? You cannot kill me."

"That maybe so, but at the very least, I can hurt you." Injis unleashed another fireball. Lu crossed her blades and absorbed the energy, she thrust the blades forwards and returned the fireball. Injis simply put out a hand and absorbed it back into her being.

"Unfortunately, my people, much like you, didn't see things my way. They restrained me, probed my mind with all the techniques they had to hand, trying to find out what went wrong. Do you know what went wrong?...Nothing! Even back then, I was who I was supposed to be, and I remain so to this day."

"Do you expect me to feel sorry for you in some way?"

"The only thing I expect from you, mortal infant, is that you stop this pitiful irritation of an attack, and die. I have returned here to do what I was born to do. I will elevate The Mora to our true standing, as rulers of this galaxy, and all other galaxies will fall under our dominion. But first, I will heal you." Injis's flame roared with ferocious intensity, she was charging up to unleash her full fury.

"No, you won't! But you will shut up! Taire, now!" shouted Lu. Taire tapped furiously on his datapad, he had isolated the signal and set a feedback loop, which he sent directly to Injis. She screamed out in pain as the signal reversed and flooded her mind. She clamped her hands to her temples. The Scavengers, now free of Injis's control, dropped to their knees, their hands held aloft in surrender. Lu seized the opportunity Taire had provided, and delivered a devastating blow to Injis's chest. It sent her reeling over the battlements, and she crashed onto the solid ground below. Lu followed her down, and made a cushioned landing with her anti-grav emitters. She stood over Injis.

"You talk too much, and The Unity will not tolerate your invasion."

"You cannot defeat me, the Unity Spire, the source of your power and inspiration, is gone. I destroyed it, and it was so easy. I really had expected more."

"You cannot destroy the Unity Spire, it is already restored. You have this all wrong; we possess the power. The Unity Spire is just one of our many tools that assists us in channelling our power - to protect The Unity from the likes of you."

* * * * * * * * * * * * * *

Targole continued his fight with Vrex. Tam and Treelo had broken free of the assault on the Gantuans, and rushed to assist him. The pair of them wielded dual energy blades. They cut and slashed at Vrex, and dodged his brutal hammer blows. Vrex swung his hammer back... Targole saw the opening...and lunged at him

viciously - it was timed to perfection.
Targole's electropike sizzled and squelched as
it plucked Vrex's eye from its socket.

"This isn't pain - pain is my friend, and
you have no idea about the excruciating levels
that I have endured. How do you think I got so
pretty?" Vrex roared with manic laughter, and
stroked his heavily-scarred face and head. It
suddenly dawned upon Tam and Treelo that Vrex
was the test subject from the recording they
had seen, back on the Gift Horse.

"I don't enjoy killing, but as it's you,
you sicko, I'll make an exception," said
Treelo, who looked like he had a vile taste in
his mouth that needed to be spat out.

"You can try, but you will fail." Vrex
slammed his pulse hammer into the ground, the
pulse energy penetrated deep into the rock.
The energy blast that followed thrusted
throughout the rock beneath them. Tam and
Targole were caught by the force of the pulse
wave. It launched them high into the air, and
they thumped back down hard on the unrelenting
rock. In that moment, Tam felt truly grateful
for his body armour. In the meantime, Treelo
had made a perfectly timed leap. His feet left
the ground before the energy pulse struck. He
threw himself forward and slashed wildly at
Vrex. He dodged the first two swipes, but the
third hit it's mark, and relieved Vrex of his
left hand. His pulse hammer thudded to the
ground, the severed hand still gripped the
handle. The scene was surprisingly bloodless -
the wound was cauterized by Treelo's weapon.

Vrex roared in anger, unaware that Tam had used the extreme distraction to circle behind him. He used Vrex's momentary lapse of concentration to inflict multiple slash wounds across his back. Vrex was done with this fight; he roared in frustration, and fled to the Black Palace.

"Leave him," said Targole breathlessly, "He has nowhere to go and no weapon."

Chapter 34 - Returning the Stone

Gliis stepped to the edge of the rippleless azure ocean. He pulled the leather thong loose from his neck, and clutched the rock in his lightly quivering hand. He was filled with nervous anticipation, and a healthy touch of fear. He looked around the cave and shouted,

"I am here. Tell me what I must do!" His words echoed around the vacuous space. A single word came back in reply.

"Follow." It carried no echo. The word hadn't been spoken. The gentle, hushed, tones had been sent telepathically to Gliis's mind. An open hand rose from the aquagel ocean and beckoned him. The hand looked to be formed from the aquagel itself. Gliis stepped into the blue, he had to trust this place.

"We must join," was the next instruction he heard. Gliis took the hand that had been offered, and he placed his White Rock between their palms. They linked fingers, and his hand grasped the other firmly. The contact had made the aquagel more solid, firm, and the hand

transformed into a complete being before his
eyes. Gliis and the being stood waist deep in
the aquagel, hand in hand. She smiled at him
with her translucent features.

"Kee'Pah?" he asked.

"Yes, I am with you," she spoke, with her
shining disc-like eyes, sending the words to
his mind. Gliis bound their hands together
using the leather thong of his necklace.

"Together as one Gliis, we are strong
enough to reach the flame."

"Are we going to the bottom of the ocean?"

"We are."

"How will I breathe?"

"Breathe normally as you would breathe
air, we will provide what your body needs."

They slipped into the thick blue gloop and
started to dive. Down they went, deeper and
deeper. The aquagel was so cold that it
penetrated Gliis's flesh, chilling him through
to his bones. Still they went on, descending
ever further into the gel that grew darker
with every stroke. At that moment, it was so
dense that it resembled tar more than aqua.
Gliis tightened his grip on Kee'Pah's hand,
and she squeezed back reassuringly.

"We are almost through the worst." A cyan-
blue glow penetrated the darkness ahead. The
rock pulsed between their palms, with growing
intensity the further they descended. The glow
grew brighter and brighter, it was almost
blinding in contrast to the darkness they had
just struggled their way through.

After what seemed like an age, they reached the ocean floor. Kee'Pah manipulated the aquagel majestically, to cast a dome of oxygen around them. The dome was large enough to encompass them both, and the still Flame of Mora.

"Is that more comfortable?" Kee'Pah asked. To Gliis's surprise, she spoke verbally. Her voice was sweet, almost singing the words with her melodic delivery.

"Yes, thank you." He coughed out the chunks of aquagel which had plugged his mouth and nose during the journey down here. The globules slithered across the ocean floor to re-join the main body of the substance.

"It is I who must thank you Gliis. We have waited so long for one who has a willing, open mind, and who is pure of soul, to connect with us. Now that you have come, we can fulfil our purpose and wake the Flame of Mora." Kee'Pah was only able to move around the edges of the dome. She had to maintain constant contact with the aquagel, as she was as one with the strange substance.

"How do we do that?" said Gliis, who was a little bashful at Kee'Pah's words, and the graceful dance-like movements she performed to navigate her way around the dome.

"Untie these bonds." He did as she asked. The two of them unlinked their fingers and separated their palms. A patch of pure white smoky vapour hung in the air between their palms: the rock had become the smoke from Gliis's dream.

"Gliis, you command the essence of your White Rock. Only you can re-join it with the Flame."

He moved his hand and the smoke followed. It was as if he were the conductor and the smoke was the music, dancing in the air. He let the smoke settle in his palm and gently closed his fist around it. He rested his left hand on the still flame, as if to reassure it. In truth, he felt that he was the one who needed reassuring. The flame was intimidatingly fragile in appearance, like a priceless, blown, glass sculpture that he was afraid he might break. The flame was warm to the touch. Gliis could feel the goodness housed within. He opened his right fist against the flame, and pressed with his palm. The flame relented, and Gliis pushed the smoke into its centre. The Flame of Mora pulsed... it was alive! Bolts of cyan fire flashed past Gliis, and they rushed to the flame to become one with its pulsing light. The fireballs were the beings from the aquagel ; he had freed them all, and they were restored to their natural state. Kee'Pah stood next to him and, with her translucent smile, simply said, "Thank you Gliis." With those final words, she became fire, and re-joined the Flame of Mora. Gliis's ears were filled with a creaking, groaning sound. He looked at the aquagel ocean above him. It was solidifying. Hairline cracks were spreading throughout the hardened substance. The Flame of Mora swelled, and to his surprise, ejected a flare. The flare made contact with the now crystal ocean, which in turn exploded. Chunks of blue crystal rock were sent soaring up and outwards, smashing open the ceiling of the cave, which had already been weakened from above by the pounding of Vrex's pulse hammer. The huge chunks of blue crystal crashed back down, and came to rest on the vast, subterranean, white rock beach.

The ceiling breach was so massive that Gliis could see the sky and the vicious, jagged, battlements of the Black Palace. The blood-curdling noise of battle raged from above. He needed to get up there to help.

"Come with me Gliis." He turned around to be greeted with the sight of a beautiful young Mora.

"Kee'Pah?" he asked.

"Yes," she smiled. She was stunningly beautiful, and carried an air of kindness and purity.

"We must get to safety before the Homecoming."

"The Homecoming?"

"Don't worry, I will explain everything, but right now we must move." Gliis couldn't stop looking at her, he was totally captivated.

"But the battle, I need to help."

"This battle will soon be won." Kee'Pah clutched Gliis's hand, and led him towards the steep steps that were carved into the walls of the ocean cave.

Chapter 35 - Above Exhilar Part 2

The Slaavene followed Tecta's order and engaged reverse thrusters. They continued their relentless bombardment as they backed smoothly away. Only the shielded Unity ships now stood directly in the path of the monstrous battering ram.

"Here goes, let's give it everything we have left. Unity fleet, execute spray formation three-six-zero. Target the breaches that the Pilots have created, and give no quarter. For peace!" yelled Tecta.

At the precise moment the command had left Tecta's mouth, an unknown ship of monstrous proportions materialised. Its appearance had caused no spatial disruption or fluctuations, which meant it hadn't dropped out of hyperspace. The only logical conclusion was that it must have disengaged some kind of cloaking tech. With the ship's arrival, the space battle ground to a sudden halt. The enormous craft emitted an energy pulse that disabled Injis's battering ram, blaster bolts and torpedoes. They appeared to be frozen in time. The Unity fleet however, were unaffected. Tecta was unsure whether this was another feature of the diamond-shielding, or the will of the massive ship. He ordered the fleet to hold fire until the mammoth vessel's intentions were clear.

"Who are they?" Zendara already knew the answer to her question, but Tecta confirmed it.

"I do not know. If this is her backup fleet, then this war is over, and The Unity is finished," he spoke grimly, as he and his crew watched on, awestruck from the bridge of The Hope.

They marvelled at the pure-white, gargantuan starship that had materialised before their eyes. The craft dominated the sky over Exhilar. It dwarfed the planet, completely blocking out the sun, to leave it in an eerie, unnatural shadow. The craft was a mobile metropolis - the size of a small planet. The sheer volume of the vessel could not be overestimated. The Unity ships and Injis's fleet resembled a swarm of midges, hovering in the face of a super moon. An intense quiver ran through The Hope and her crew. They were being scanned. The scans were followed by a blinding burst of brilliant white light, it bleached out everything. When the glare receded, and their vision readjusted, Injis's fleet was in the throes of decimation. The

White Rocks had been called home - like deadly flocks of homing grooks they returned; crashing through the battering ram of Injis's ships, until they were pummelled to nothing but cosmic dust.

The Unity ships remained intact, and completely untouched. Tecta's instincts regarding the giant ship appeared to have been right… so far.

Chapter 36 – The Order of the White Rock

The Scavengers were free of Injis's mind control. They turned on her, and joined the R'aal and Unitians in baying for her blood.

"Stop!" shouted Lu, "We are not animals, we will not treat her like a sideshow spectacle. Despite all that she has done, she is still a sentient being, and the correct justice will be served. Not by us, but by those from which she came." Injis clambered to her feet

"Weak fools! You cannot defeat me. You have no killer instinct." As soon as those words left her cruel bony lips, a single white rock hurtled from the sky and struck her on the skull. She looked skyward, dazed. A ferocious barrage of rocks followed; they knocked her from her feet, and her battered body was forced backwards through the chasm that had been the ceiling of the ocean cave. She seemed to fall in slow motion. Rocks still slammed against her from all directions. She crashed onto the unrelenting rocky beach below, her body limp and broken. The White Rock continued to rain down, crushing and burying her, suffocating her flame.

That which she thought would be her saviour, had turned out to be her downfall. So arrogant was she, that she refused to believe that she could be betrayed. She had thought that freeing the Flame would allow her to build a new order; but she had been betrayed by the key element of her own plan. Lu, Tam, Treelo, Taire and Targole all peered over the edge of the chasm. The pile of White Rock was so high, it had formed a bank that stretched from the beach all the way up to the breach where they stood.

Vrex stood at the top of the Black Palace. He had watched everything unfold with his remaining eye. The Hornets tore through the cloud deck above him, and screamed into the tunnels, heading for the Loway. Enough was enough, he knew what being on the losing side felt like, and there was no coming back from this, not even for Injis.

"I will honour you, Injis," he shouted, as he entered The Vengeance and powered up the engines. At the point of lift off, Pilot's Hornet ripped through the Black Palace. He had doubled back after he spotted The Vengeance on the palace roof. His drill ship bored up through the palace and tore The Vengeance's tail section clean off.

"Pilot stop you, ugly bad man!" Pilot

butted out, as he made his attack run. The Vengeance launch sequence was already complete, the lateral boosters engaged. The Vengeance spiralled into the sky in a chaotic corkscrew motion, on a course to who knows where.

* * * * * * * * * * *

Kee'Pah and Gliis approached, escorted by the, (thankfully unharmed), Seventeen and Zero-Nine. Taire was relieved to see the Protectors, alive and well. His shielding, (despite his own misgivings), had done its job. The droids approached him.

"Don't sweat it Taire, you have made us impenetrable," Zero laughed, and slapped him on the back a little too forcefully.

"I never doubted your shielding for a second Taire. **T**hank you." said Seventeen as they entered the crowd, those gathered at the breach parted, to permit Kee'Pah access to the defeated Injis. Kee'Pah stood atop the mountain of White Rock that had restrained her and shouted,

"Injis, shamed daughter of The Mora. We are the Order of the White Rock, guardians of the Flame of Mora, and you... you are nothing more than an anomaly. A relic from a long-forgotten time. There is no place for you in the here and now. We have learned that in order to understand life, we must understand and embrace all its aspects, including death.

We must abide by natural law. Yes, you killed, but you could not appreciate what you had taken from others, because you are an immortal being. With your 'healing,' all you have achieved is the theft of the only things that any mortals has. Their hope and their life itself. We have come to understand that the quest to stop death is a fool's errand, embarked upon by our ancestors in shame of your actions. We had lost our way because of you.

Now we are reborn with renewed purpose. We have watched through the stolen rocks for millennia, watched this universe grow, destroy itself, and then grow again. The one constant that we have observed is the mortal's primal instinct to survive. The Hushed failed to crush their spirit, as have you, and The Dawn Wars will always be a testament to this instinct of survival. The true, natural path to immortality is through family and our actions - to live on in the hearts and minds of friends and loved ones, and the generations yet to come. We are evolved, and we have chosen to become mortal. We are reborn as true healers once more. We will not tolerate your attempts to reign in terror or sully our ancestor's legacy any further. Your vapid existence is at an end. We are ready to join the peoples of The Unity, in harmony as equals, if they will accept us. And you Injis, you will go back to the darkness from which you came." Kee'Pah looked to the sky.

"NO, HER DEATH IS MINE TO CLAIM!" a livid
voice roared from below - it was Kalto. He had
found a way down onto the beach. He held aloft
a gigantic boulder - he meant to smash Injis's
exposed head. He towered over her, with the
unquenchable fire of hatred in his eyes.
Injis's own dimly-lit eyes peered out from the
mountain of stone that restrained her. Her
inner fire was all but snuffed out.

"She will be dealt with by the ancients,"
shouted Kee'Pah, as she gestured to the sky.

"No, I must avenge Shrimp. I promised
him." Kalto appeared to be frozen on the spot,
he shook with rage and raw emotion. The
boulder exploded in his hands. His eyes grew
wide and his mouth dropped open. Seventeen had
blasted the boulder to dust, and Zero stood on
the opposite side of Kalto, wrist blasters
trained on him. A vast shadow lingered over
the fractured landscape of Exhilar. The eerie
semi-darkness gave the impression of a total
solar eclipse. Kalto shook himself back into
the present moment.

"I just have one thing I need to say to
her." He knelt next to Injis's exposed head.

"Shrimp's revenge will be had. I may not
get to kill you, but I will find Vrex, and end
any hope of your legacy ever being reborn," he
whispered, through gritted teeth, with hushed
venom.
The black smoke that smouldered in Injis's
eyes sensed Kalto's proximity and his pure
rage. He was completely unaware of the smoke
as it stealthily entered his nostrils. It was

a devious, intelligent substance, and it would bide its time, laying dormant in its oblivious new host...for now. He stood defiantly and spat down on her defeated face, the foamy saliva made a satisfying hiss on contact.

"I'm done." He held his hands aloft and looked at Seventeen, who gave the slightest nod. Kalto turned and walked towards the steps. Injis's spent body dematerialised before their eyes. She was once again a captive on the Mora ship that dominated the skies above them.

Chapter 37 - Restoration

A youthful looking, middle-aged woman stepped out from the entrance to the subterranean cave system. She was familiar and radiant.

"We must get to the higher ground, the planet commands us."

"She is right, The Mora are beginning the restoration," added Kee'Pah, half excited and half afraid.

"Who are you?" Taire asked the woman suspiciously, but Gliis recognised her.

"Vrin? How can this be?" Those who knew Vrin were stunned.

"This is impossible," said Targole.

"If I've learned anything since jumping on this crazy train, it's that anything is possible my friend, and she is smokin' hot... is that weird?" Treelo was a changed man, but not that changed.

"Yes," Targole replied, bluntly.

"Your instincts Gliis, as always, are spot on. There will be time to figure this out later," Vrin replied to Gliis's earlier question.

"You heard Vrin," shouted Lu, "Let's move, now." She led the way, weaving through the crevices and outcrops of the harsh terrain. The mammoth Mora ship began a deep throbbing hum that rumbled through the ground beneath them. The chunks of blue aquagel that were scattered about the caved beach, melted into liquid water. The liquid swelled and gathered momentum, as it flooded the ocean floor and started to rise. The Flame of Mora burned with increasing intensity, and the brighter it burned, the more the water expanded. Soon it had reached the massive breach where the roof of the ocean cave had once been. The water carried the White Rocks with it, as it rushed from the cave systems and cleansed what had been, moments before, a blood-soaked battlefield.

The Siblings, their friends, allies and what remained of the Scavengers, watched in anxious wonder as a miracle unfolded. They had scaled Exhilar's mountainous terrain and reached its highest point, in the hope that it was high enough. The water and rock still rose, creeping ever closer to them, then the swell abruptly stopped. The planet was transformed; it was as if it had been turned inside out. Where there had been barren, black, volcanic wasteland, there were now vast, expansive,

White Rock beaches. They stretched for miles in all directions. An endless, sparkling, azure ocean, rippled and lapped at the brilliant white shorelines. The early evening sun danced in the sparkles on the surface of the water. They began to step tentatively from the remnants of the rocky black outcrops, and onto the immaculate white-wash of beach. The vulgar black rock receded into the ground, to be replaced by the familiar sight of the Core Loway pod.

"Wow, what happen here?" asked Pilot, as he emerged. He looked at Tam, "Dis you again, Friend Tam?"

"Not this time Pilot," he gestured to Kee'Pah.

"Welcome to Phamora," she said with a beaming smile.
The Order of the White Rock rose from the shallows, glistening in breath-taking white and blue tones. They made their way onto the beach where they stopped, dropped to one knee, and bowed toward the Siblings.

"Please rise," said Lu gently, "We owe you a debt of gratitude. You are truly a people of The Unity, and we would be honoured if you would join with us."

"The honour would be ours," answered Kee'Pah, on behalf of her people. She looked skyward and wore a beautiful serene smile.

The Mora ship powered up, and with a high-pitched whine, it was gone, vanishing from the skies above. The welcome sight of The Unity fleet filled the void that the giant vessel had left. The ships descended triumphantly. Pilot's squadron of recharged Hornets put on a dizzying display of celebratory aerobatics, drawing cheers of jubilation from the exhausted (but exhilarated) survivors, who gathered together on the beach.

"Gliis, my purpose here is fulfilled. The White Rock - your White Rock - was always destined to be mine, and now finally we are joined as one. Although I am no longer purely your rock, I would still very much like to be yours." He blushed and smiled. Kee'Pah continued to speak.

"You are no longer the only unique being in the galaxy, I am now unique too. The first Mora with the ability to age and grow, free of my cast. I choose you Gliis, for my companion and teacher. Are you willing to teach me the ways of this galaxy?"

"I am still learning the ways of the galaxy myself," he replied.

"So, we can learn together maybe?" asked Kee'Pah.

"I'd like that very much," he replied. Gliis looked to Lu, who had been deep in conversation with Vrin. She stroked her youthful face in wonder. Both sensed his eyes on them, and looked over to him. Vrin's now youthful face beamed radiantly, while Lu gave her brother a knowing nod and a smile.

"Besides," he said, turning his attention back to Kee'Pah, "You are the fifth child of The Unity. You are destined to be with us."

Chapter 38 - The Seeker

A dart-like vessel pierced the light grey sky, and made a swift descent to the icy planet's surface. The sleek vessel was clearly of Raktarian design, finished in highly-reflective chrome and translucent red. The ship's immaculately polished surface reflected the planet's glacial terrain in spectacular detail. A sharp hiss sounded, and a concealed door opened in the side of the craft. It transformed seamlessly to become a boarding ramp. A tall figure stepped out from the doorway, and pulled up the faux fur hood of his bulky padded jacket, in order to protect his head and face from the wind and cold. His heavy boots made a metallic clang with every footfall, as he walked the length of the ramp to reach terra firmer. The crunch and squeak of thick snow underfoot was a brand-new experience, as were the flurries of light snow that continued to whip around him.

Five frustrating years had passed, and Taire was no closer to finding the sixth child of

The Unity. Once the dust had settled on the battle of Mora, Tecta had exiled himself. Since he had given the command to use Feer'aal to better The Unity's chances of beating Injis, he had felt like more of a risk than a benefit to the fledgling Unity. He had never thought of himself as being capable of such extremes. Tecta had broken his own rules, and believed that he had condemned his cybernetic soul to damnation. He even compared himself to Injis and Rarvin. He alone was of this opinion; the rest of the new Unity knew that he had done what was necessary to protect them, and if he hadn't of taken those actions, it was highly doubtful that any of them would still be alive today.

His father figure's sudden disappearance had deeply affected Taire down to his core, even more so than it had his siblings. Taire still had the Sixth to find, and Tecta had always been there to be his friend, mentor and confidant. Now Lu and Gliis had additional companions in Tam and Kee'Pah respectively, he felt more alone than ever before. He needed Tecta's guidance desperately, but Tecta wasn't here. He was out there alone, and unreachable, enduring his self-imposed exile in the vast expanse of space.

Taire had followed Etala's advice, and took it upon himself to search for the answers, but he had repeatedly drawn a complete blank. In the years since the activation of the Unity Spire,

Taire had avoided coming to Raktar. Although it was his native planet, he'd never felt the urge, or the calling, to come here before. He had exhausted all other avenues. In a fit of hope and desperation, he had concluded that, in order to find the answer within himself, he needed to know more about himself, his people and his heritage. He needed to find out who Taire truly was. An electronic trilling sounded to his right-hand side, it was the now familiar complaining of Clint, his self-manufactured companion. The name Clint was an abbreviation of the tech he had been built around. **C**onscious **L**earn**IN**g **T**echnology. Clint had strayed out of his depth in the thick snow. His boosters roared like miniature blow torches. They melted the surrounding snow, and lifted him above the drift, onto the comparative safety of the boarding ramp. He landed with a gentle clank, and trilled some more.

"Yes Clint, I know it's cold, stop complaining. I programmed you to be my companion and sounding board, not a nagging stand-in for a life partner." Clint gave a negative bleep.

"Fine, you just sulk. I didn't have to bring you along. You insisted, remember?" Clint gave a blunt *nurng* sound, hovered up to Taire's kit bag, and nestled himself inside.

"*Sorry?* So you should be." Taire couldn't quite believe that it had come to this. He had receded so far into himself that he had resorted to building a companion, rather than be around people. He knew Lu, Gliis, Tam and Kee'Pah hadn't meant to exclude him, and a large part of the problem was that he had distanced himself from them, and had gotten lost in his introverted search for the Sixth. However, he had grown very fond of Clint, and although at times he infuriated him, he did provide companionship and a welcome distraction. As Taire regarded his surroundings, he rubbed his hands together to create some warming friction. He had purposefully chosen this spot to land his ship. He had it on good authority that this was the most accessible landing platform on Raktar; his current semi-frozen state had caused him to question the reliability of his sources. It was clear to see - there was nothing here. No dwellings or research sites, no people, just the crunch of the snow, and the howl and whistle of the wind that hurried the gentle flakes of snow about the icy outcrops.

Taire was startled by a sudden jolt underfoot, and it was accompanied by a new sound. The sound was mechanical, it resembled the grinding of heavy gear plates. Taire became aware of the sensation of motion. He, Clint and his ship were being slowly rotated and lowered into the planet's surface. Clint gave a panicked trill.

 "Don't worry little friend, these are my people."

The End

This book is dedicated to the memory of my father in-law Paul Mann. Loved and missed by us all always.

Thank you to my wife, my children, family and friends for all of your support, and to anyone who has read my books, lots of love x

Cover art by Graham Mann

The Unity Chronicles
will continue

Book Three

The Lost Protector

Printed in Poland
by Amazon Fulfillment
Poland Sp. z o.o., Wrocław